MICHAEL GRANT

THE
MAGNIFICENT
12

BOOK TWO

THE TRAP

KT KATHERINE TEGEN BOOKS
An Imprint of HarperCollins Publishers

Katherine Tegen Books is an imprint of HarperCollins Publishers.

The Magnificent 12: The Trap

Library of Congress Cataloging-in-Publication Data
Grant, Michael.
   The trap / Michael Grant. — 1st ed.
      p.   cm. — (The Magnificent 12 ; 2)
   Summary: Mack MacAvoy, an average-seeming twelve-year-old boy who happens to have special powers, travels to China in an effort to assemble an elite team of his peers to help him thwart the evil Pale Queen.
   ISBN 978-0-06-183369-4
   [1. Fantasy.   2. Adventure and adventurers—Fiction.   3. Good and evil—Fiction.   4. Humorous stories.]   I. Title.
PZ7.G7671Tr   2011   2010040580
[Fic]— dc22   CIP
                                                                           AC

Typography by Amy Ryan
12 13 14 15 16   LP/BR   10 9 8 7 6 5 4 3 2 1
❖
First paperback edition, 2012

For Katherine, Jake, and Julia

BOOK TWO

THE TRAP

Before Chapter One

Grimluk—looking as grim as ever—said the following while appearing as an indistinct image in a shiny chrome object in a bathroom in Sydney, Australia:

"I cannot guide you much further, Mack of the Magnifica. You must learn the secrets of this world. Find the ancient ones . . . the great forgotten forces. Some will help you. Some . . . not so much. But above all: Learn the ways of Vargran! Assemble the

Twelve!! Time is shooooort!!!"

Grimluk usually didn't use that many exclamation points. Nor did he typically draw a word out that way by adding unnecessary vowels. He tended to be grim rather than excited. So Mack paid close attention. This involved leaning nearer to the shiny chrome object in question, which if you've ever been in a public restroom, you'll know is not considered appropriate behavior.

"How short?" Mack asked.

"Short. Very shooooort."

"But I mean, like, days? Weeks?"

"Thirty-six days from today is the end of the three thousand years of the Pale Queen's sentence of banishment. The spell that binds her—already weakened—will end. And she will be free."

"Say what? You're telling me I have thirty-six days to find all the Magnificent Twelve? It's just two of us so far! We're just the Magnificent Two!"

"Thirty-six days to assemble the Twelve and destroy the Pale Queen!"

"You didn't think to mention this earlier?"

"I didn't have my calendar handy." Then Grimluk's

wrinkled, haggard, drawn, worn, not-exactly-cute-little-Justin-Bieber face frowned. He rolled his white eyes up as though trying to remember. "Wait," he said. "It's thirty-five, not thirty-six. I always get seven minus four wrong."

"I've already lost a day?" Mack shrilled.

"Go to the nine dragons of Daidu," Grimluk whispered.

To which Mack replied, "The what?"

"Don't make me repeat myself," Grimluk snapped. "This apparition thing isn't easy. Each time I do it, I lose power. I weaken . . . I . . ."

And then he faded out. And Mack was left to stare at the chrome pipe with the same frustrated expression he got when the cable went out.

A man standing two urinals down shot him a worried look. "You all right, kid?"

"Yes, sir. Sometimes I talk to toilets. It . . . Well, they seem to like it."

"Is that so?" The man thought about it for a minute. Then he said, "Hello, toilet."

Mack was giving up on Grimluk and turning away when the ancient apparition came back into view. But now his voice was a whisper. An urgent, sketchy whisper: ". . . dragons may help . . . the Egge Rocks . . ."

"Daidu, nine dragons, egg rocks?" Mack repeated. "Egg Rocks? Is that a band?"

"Egge Rocks!" Grimluk whispered. "Teutoberg Forest. There . . . the eyes show!"

"Daidu, nine dragons, a band called Egg Rocks, toityberg . . . and an ice show?"

"Eyes!"

"Ice?"

Grimluk shook his head slowly, rolled his eyes up, and gasped, "Close enough . . ."

In a faint whisper, so quiet that Mack had to lean close—which looked extremely not-normal—Grimluk said, "Beware of . . ."

Mack listened intently and stared at the chrome for a while longer. He tried flushing a couple of times, banging on the handle on the theory that sometimes it helped to bang on things when they didn't work.

But Grimluk was gone.

Again.

Which was very inconvenient because Mack had the impression that the last word Grimluk had said was "trap." And that's the kind of word you want to hear clearly enunciated.

"Grimluk has got to get himself a phone."

It was irritating. Frustrating. Because Mack had quite a few questions.

He would have to answer those questions the hard way.

He clicked on his iPhone. Opened the browser. Opened the Google search window. And typed in *Daidu*.

One

For David MacAvoy—who all his friends called Mack—the flight to China went much better than the flight to Australia had.

The flight to Australia had ended when a beautiful shape-shifting evil princess named Ereskigal—who all her friends (she had no friends) called Risky—turned into a monster and yanked Mack out of a jet at thirty thousand feet and dropped him into the ocean.

On this flight, the one from Sydney to Shanghai,

they'd had some turbulence, the first-class bathroom ran out of hand towels, and the meal they served was fish. But none of that was quite as awful as a five-mile fall through thin, freezing air into the shark-infested Pacific. Then they had transferred in Shanghai for a flight to Beijing.

Mack was accompanied by Jarrah Major, the second member of the Magnificent Twelve. And by his former bully and current bodyguard, Stefan Marr.

Stefan could pass for an adult because although he was in the same grade as twelve-year-old Mack, he was fifteen and had the muscular development of one of those guys who sell exercise equipment on cable TV.

In case anyone asked, they were telling people that Stefan was the "big brother" of Mack and Jarrah. How a dangerously handsome, muscle-bound blond thug had become the brother of a very average-sized, average-looking kid like Mack, let alone the brother of Jarrah, who had the skin tone of her Indigenous Australian mother, was anyone's guess.

But people seldom questioned Stefan.

Certainly not more than once.

Anyway, the flight to China was relatively normal, although Mack spent the entire time gripping the arm-rest and whimpering. He had no fear of flying but he had a morbid fear of oceans and of sharks, and there's a lot of ocean between Australia and China.

At one point Stefan smacked Mack on the head to get Mack to whimper more quietly. Mack didn't really resent this much because if Stefan hadn't done it, the rest of the passengers seated nearby would have. There's just something about a sweating, trembling, teeth-gritting, seat-gripping, weeping, I-don't-want-to-die-whining kid that gets on people's nerves.

But now Mack, Jarrah, and Stefan were off the plane and at the Beijing airport waiting for their luggage to come down the conveyor belt. They were surrounded by passengers who'd been on the plane from Australia with them. Everyone was bleary and tired and leaning on luggage carts and checking their watches and trying to get more bars on their cell phones.

And standing well apart from Mack.

Mack was thumbing through the Chinese currency he'd gotten from an ATM upon landing.

"I don't understand this money. I'm going to end

up paying someone a hundred dollars for a soda," Mack muttered.

And that's when Stefan poked him. "Dude," Stefan said. "Over there."

A very old man, dressed almost entirely in green, was coming toward them. He was still a hundred yards away and did not move briskly. So Mack had plenty of time to say, "Paddy 'Nine Iron' Trout? Here?"

"Paddy Wacky," Stefan growled. He smiled then and interlaced his fingers in order to crack his knuckles and stretch his arm muscles. Stefan knew that before you engaged in the strenuous activity of beating someone up, it's best to stretch. It saves you getting cramps in your biceps.

www.themag12.com

"You know that old git?" Jarrah asked.

"He's a Nafia hit man," Mack said.

"What? Mafia, like Tony Soprano?"

"Not Mafia. Nafia," Mack said.

"Ah," Jarrah said, as though that clarified the situation for her. (It didn't.)

Mack looked for his bag. There were plenty of bags

going by slowly on the carousel, but none were his. Annoying, because if the bag were there, he'd have time to pick it up, place it on the luggage cart along with Jarrah's backpack and Stefan's bag, and leave at a leisurely pace.

Paddy "Nine Iron" Trout? Not a fast-moving guy.

But Mack knew about the sword in Nine Iron's walking stick. So although Nine Iron was probably almost a hundred years old and therefore slow, slow, slooooow, you didn't necessarily want to hang around and wait for him. If you stood still long enough, he would absolutely stab you.

"You want me to go beat him up?" Stefan asked, with the kind of hopeful expression you might see on the face of an eager puppy who thinks you have Pup-Peroni.

"Not unless he starts something," Mack said. "How would you explain it to the cops? You can't just beat up a hundred-year-old guy."

Nine Iron made his way to the far side of the carousel. He stood there like any other person waiting for a bag. Except that as he stood there, he stared with sunken, bleary, borderline-crazy eyes at Mack.

Mack almost felt he should wave.

Apparently Nine Iron spotted the bag he was waiting for. It had a jaunty plaid pattern. Nine Iron leaned over and struggled to grab it. Except no, no, he wasn't really trying to grab it. He was . . .

Mack heard the sound of a zipper.

Nine Iron smiled, revealing teeth like those of an unhealthy horse. He laughed, a creaky sound filled with malice.

"I warned you not to—" he said, but then held up a finger, indicating he needed a moment. He reached inside his green blazer and pulled out a clear plastic tube and mouthpiece.

Nine Iron sucked oxygen once, twice, three times.

"—defy me!" Nine Iron finished.

The plaid bag came around the carousel. Unzipped.

It popped open! The top was pushed back by a tiny, scabby hand that appeared to be missing a couple of fingers.

As Mack saw the contents of the suitcase, he squealed. So did Jarrah. So, actually, did Stefan. Not squeals of delight. More like squeals of "Eeew!"

"Ah-ha-ha!" Nine Iron cackled. "Arise, my

Lepercons! Arise and—"

He paused to take several more deep breaths from his oxygen tank while everyone—Mack, Jarrah, Stefan, and the Lepercons—waited.

" —kill! Kill for the Pale Queen!"

The suitcase was full of what were definitely living things, but not like any living things Mack had ever seen before. They were about the size of fat house cats. They were more or less human shaped, but with legs too long for their bodies. They didn't wear clothing, but their torsos were discreetly covered by black-on-white spotted fur.

They looked a little like dalmatian puppies. Except not cute. The Lepercons didn't make you want to say "Aaaw"; they made you want to say "Aaah!" Largely because they had leprous, disfigured faces that reminded Mack of wadded-up gym socks with down-turned doll mouths.

They appeared to have started life with the usual number of fingers and toes and noses, but the bare flesh visible beyond the fur was all eaten at, chewed up, and missing things that ought to be there.

"Did he say leprechauns?" Jarrah asked.

"Lepercons, you stupid—" Nine Iron squinted. He growled. "Who are you, anyway?"

"Jarrah Major," she answered. "Pleased to . . . Well, maybe not."

There looked to be about a dozen of the Lepercons packed into the suitcase like sardines. Diseased, unhealthy sardines.

They unpacked themselves very quickly.

And Nine Iron laughed again as he unzipped a second plaid suitcase.

Lepercons leaped from both suitcases.

They leaped, and paused there for a moment on the carousel to unzip an outer pocket on each suitcase. From which they extracted bundles of sharp implements like knitting needles, handed them around, and then, armed, they launched themselves at Mack, Jarrah, and Stefan.

Two

Mack did the smart thing, the thing anyone would do when attacked by a dozen knitting-needle-wielding, diseased minipeople who looked like dalmatian puppies with mismatched fingers and deformed legs.

He yelled, "Yaa-ah-aaah!" And ran.

The Lepercons were quick. At least, the ones who still had both feet were. Some were chasing him on stumps. Or on one stump and one regular foot. Or on one whole leg and a partial leg.

These were slower.

Mack felt a needle jab the back of his left calf. It didn't penetrate his jeans, but it hurt and he yelled, "Hey, cut it out!"

Because normally that works.

A second jab caught him in the right butt cheek.

Mack spotted a small woman hauling a large wheeled suitcase. He snatched the bag, yelled, "Sorry!" then executed a running pivot and flung the suitcase at the charging Lepercons.

Three of them went down like bowling pins and let out howls of outrage.

"*Agara! Agara! Agara!*" Which is probably the traditional Lepercon howl of outrage.

But the others leaped clear of the bag and were all over Mack in a heartbeat.

Knitting needles jabbed at jeans and T-shirt without much effect, but one caught him in the palm of his left hand, and that drew blood.

A particularly persistent Lepercon climbed onto Mack's shoulders from behind. He felt the tip of the needle enter his ear. He jerked away, but the needle jabbed, jabbed, jabbed again.

"Hey! That hurts!"

Mack reached around, grabbed a handful of spotted fur, and yanked the creature up over his head. He held him by one leg and swung the little monster like a club, beating at the others.

Thumpf!

Mack nailed one of the Lepercons pretty well, but then the leg he was holding came off—just detached. He stared stupidly at it. There was no blood, no hanging arteries or gore.

In fact, the detached end of the leg looked like a piece of well-aged blue cheese. Possibly Stilton.

Although it may have been Gorgonzola.

Mack wanted to throw up. It wasn't a good thing to see. Or smell. And if it was blue cheese . . . No. No, it couldn't be! He hated blue cheese. Worse yet: he had a deep and awful terror of blue cheese.

"Jasnafar's been legged!" one of the Lepercons screeched.

"Avenge Jasnafar!"

"Agara! Agara!" the now one-legged Jasnafar cried. He hopped on his remaining leg, oozing gooey blue

cheeselike product from his stump, and stabbed busily at Mack's foot.

"Get off me, get off me!" Mack cried. "Noooo, nooooo! Get it off me! Nooooo, it's Roquefort!"

Jarrah and Stefan were both busy with their own Lepercon problems. Mack caught a flash of Jarrah tossing a Lepercon so hard it went spinning across the floor and smacked into a Chinese boy, who kicked it away with a reflexive soccer kick.

Stefan had one of the Lepercons in his teeth. He chomped down hard and spit out a Lepercon hand. Stefan also had a knitting needle either stuck into his head or his hair—hopefully his hair—and was too busy to run to Mack's rescue.

"You fools!" Nine Iron cried. "Go for the boy! The boy!"

The old man had to sit down after that and inhale more oxygen from the tube. He sat on the carousel and was swept slowly away, wedged in between a large black garment bag and a gray duffel bag.

Mack punched one of the Lepercons. Right in the face.

Pumpf!

Blue cheese product shot from the creature's nose, mouth, and ears.

Mack felt a sharp pain. The knitting needle just sat there, sticking out of his neck. "Hey!" he yelled.

He snatched the needle out and stared at the single drop of his own blood.

Now Mack was mad as well as terrified. "Okay, that's enough!"

In one fluid movement he jammed the needle into the nearest Lepercon. It went easily all the way through. Goo squeezed out around the puncture.

Mack kicked, punched, and generally flailed away like a panicky kid in the midst of a phobia meltdown— although it was all very Mortal Kombat in his head. But flailing didn't help much, and now more of the Lepercons were heeding Nine Iron's fading, wheezing shouts and leaving Jarrah and Stefan in order to come after Mack. They were all over him. The sheer weight of them made him stagger.

But worse was the morbid terror of the goo oozing from the Lepercons' many wounds.

Mack suffered from twenty-one known phobias— unreasonable fears. We don't have time to list them all, but they ran the gamut from fear of puppets to a fear of fear itself, which is called phobophobia.

The thing with phobias is that they aren't reasonable fears, such as a fear of clowns or brussels sprouts or reality shows. Phobias are at a whole different level. The phobia panic builds and builds until pretty soon a person just loses it altogether.

And that's what was happening to Mack. The grossness of the blue cheese goo—the unbelievable disgustingness of it, the football player's armpit smell of it—was working on the scared little monkey brain buried deep down inside Mack's otherwise pretty cool human brain.

Of course the phobia thing wouldn't be a problem if he were dead. In minutes, if not seconds, one of the needles would hit an artery or an eyeball or go in through Mack's ear. He realized then that this wasn't just a fight: it was life and death.

There were words Mack could use, Vargran words, that could freeze time and let him escape. But it was hard to think of them when a dozen evil midgets were jabbing you with needles and when a sick fear was dumping all sorts of panic chemicals into your system.

Then it came to him! He knew the Vargran command. It was *ret click-ur*.

Not that hard to say, except that just as he was forming the words, a needle jabbed him in the gum. It wasn't that hard a hit; it just scraped his gum. It didn't knock out a tooth or anything, but the Lepercon wasn't backing away. He had hold of Mack's shirt with one hand and had hauled himself up onto Mack's chest, and with his free hand he was trying to shove the knitting needle right down Mack's throat.

Mack bit down hard on the needle. He held it tight with his going-to-need-braces-in-a-few-years teeth.

He tried to pull the Lepercon away, but the thing was swarming him. At least six of the things were on his body, hauling at him, grabbing handfuls of shirt and hair, using belt, nose, and ears as climbing grips.

And smelling like a hobo's sneakers.

The needle scraped against Mack's teeth. If he opened his mouth to say the spell, he would die.

"Esk-ma belast!"

But it wasn't Mack who said this; it was Jarrah.

She was a mess, hair all askew, and somewhat covered in Lepercon goo. She looked scared, wild, and furious.

Stefan stomped a heel onto one of the Lepercons, which popped like a noxious water balloon. He yanked the needle out of his hair, laughed happily—this was Stefan's idea of a party—and ran (finally!) to help Mack.

But Mack didn't need as much help anymore. The Lepercon on his shoulder fell heavily to the ground. The one on his chest—the one trying to jab a knitting needle down his throat—was changing. The small, wrinkled ShamWow face was becoming smoother, bigger, fuller. The wrinkles were filling in. Plumping.

Mack felt the weight of the creature grow. He felt his shirt stretch farther and farther until the Lepercon lost his grip and slid, moaning (*"Agara . . . agara . . ."*), to the floor.

Mack glanced wildly around. All the Lepercons were growing. Larger. Heavier. They were no longer the size of fat cats; they were the size of moderately full garbage bags. And still growing.

They were not moving much.

The needles looked tiny now in their bratwurst-sized fingers.

Mack spit the needle out of his mouth and said, "Whoa."

"Huh," Stefan remarked. He seemed disappointed.

Jarrah, looking shell-shocked, came to them. The Lepercons were now the size of cows. Stunned bystanders stared in awe and horror. Some took pictures with their cell phones. YouTube would be getting some very odd uploads. Thumbs flew across touch screens: Twitter was getting the news out.

Other folks stolidly wheeled their luggage past as though the problem of rapidly enlarging, leprous, cheese-stuffed monsters was just another obstacle to be overcome by the weary traveling public.

"What did you do?" Mack asked Jarrah, panting.

"It was all I could think of. I don't know that much Vargran," Jarrah said. "I was trying to say 'follow.' I was going to lead them away."

"They would have killed you," Mack said.

"Eh," Jarrah said. "They might have tried."

Mack intercepted an admiring look from Stefan. Jarrah was his kind of girl.

"I think what I actually said must have been 'grow,' not 'follow.' 'Grow monster.'"

"'Grow monster'?"

Jarrah looked sheepish. "Yeah, that could have gone badly, eh?"

The Lepercons were still getting bigger. In fact, they were crowding the baggage area. Lepercons weren't built to be the size of parade balloons, so they were as helpless as slugs. Big, giant slugs.

"*Agara!*" the one-legged Lepercon slurred.

"Yeah? *Agara* you, you big fat scab!" Jarrah snapped.

Mack spotted his bag on the carousel. He snagged it and wedged it onto the luggage cart along with Jarrah's and Stefan's luggage.

Nine Iron was just coming around on the carousel, still wedged between a garment bag and a duffel.

"You wait right there!" Nine Iron raged. "I'm coming for—"

He paused. Fumbled for his plastic mouthpiece. Breathed. Breathed.

Breathed.

Breathed.

"—you!"

Mack was breathing as hard as Nine Iron. The fear of death was gone, but he was now surrounded by what had to be a thousand pounds of warm blue cheese or a blue cheeselike product.

Nine Iron was struggling to get up off the carousel, but he was sitting kind of far down, with his legs over the side, so he had to use his walking stick to get himself up. Unfortunately, since Nine Iron was moving, the floor was also moving, and he couldn't get the stick . . . Well, you get the picture.

"Do you have any idea what Lepercons cost?" Nine Iron cried.

"Leave me alone, you crazy old man!" Mack yelled.

"I'll follow you to—"

He breathed. Breathed.

And then the carousel ran Nine Iron straight into the engorging, growing, swelling, bloated butt cheek of a massive Lepercon.

So Mack didn't hear where exactly Nine Iron was going to follow him. He just heard a sort of angry "Mmmphh mmmph!"

"Let's get out of here," Jarrah said. "Place smells."

"Blueturophobia," Mack said. "It's a fear of blue cheese."

"Are you going to have one of your crazy fits?" Stefan asked.

"Not if you knock me out, throw me in a taxi, and don't wake me up until I'm standing in a shower," Mack said.

Five seconds later Mack was draped over the luggage. Stefan wheeled him—blissfully unconscious—toward the exit.

Three

Now we'll explain all the stuff we didn't explain earlier. It's called "exposition." Toss that word into the middle of your next English class. Your teacher will be like, "Wow, someone is actually paying attention!" That will be kind of sad, really.

David "Mack" MacAvoy was a normal-looking kid living a normal life in the almost normal city of Sedona, Arizona. He had no idea that he would be called upon to save the world from a terrible evil.

A terrible evil no one had actually heard of.

Everyone expects the world to eventually be destroyed by some combination of global warming, a giant asteroid strike, the sun going supernova, the planet falling off its axis, a wandering black hole, the explosion of the giant magma-filled zit below Yellowstone— Oh, you hadn't heard about that? Well, it's best not to think about it—or a rapidly spreading disease that turns people into flesh-eating zombies.

Asteroids, exploding sun, global warming, black hole, magma pimple, and zombie apocalypse—those are all happening for sure. Those are the things we know about.

But in the twenty-first century absolutely no one was worrying about the imminent release of the Pale Queen from the World Beneath, where she'd been imprisoned for three thousand years.

It's always the thing you're not worrying about that gets you. You'd think Mack would have realized that before most. After all, Mack suffered from a whole long list of phobias.

He had arachnophobia, fear of spiders. Dentophobia,

fear of dentists. Pyrophobia, fear of fire (which was ironic considering he'd used a Vargran spell to turn into a sort of minisun while fighting Ereskigal at one point).

He had pupaphobia, fear of puppets; trypano-phobia, fear of getting shots; thalassophobia, fear of oceans—which led fairly naturally to selachophobia, fear of sharks.

And as mentioned earlier, phobophobia, which is the fear of developing more fears.

The mother of all fears for Mack was claustropho-bia, fear of small, enclosed spaces. Of being buried alive. Not that anyone would exactly enjoy that, but Mack could freak out just thinking about it.

But despite his close relationship with fear, Mack hadn't known there was a Pale Queen about to be released from the World Beneath.

(By the way, if you know all this because you read the first book? You can skip this chapter and go to the next one. My feelings won't be hurt.)

Mack's part in that three-thousand-year-old story began when he was about to get the snot—excuse me, mucus—beaten out of him by Stefan Marr, King of All Bullies at Richard Gere Middle School. (Go, Fighting Pupfish!)

Just as the beating was scheduled to start, Grimluk appeared. Ghostlike. Special effects time. Booga booga.

Grimluk's appearance froze time for a few seconds while he began to lay out the bad news for Mack. In effect, "Dude, you are one of a select group called the Magnificent Twelve. You need to drop out of school, assemble the rest of the Magnifica from the four corners of the Earth, learn this magic language called Vargran, and take down the Pale Queen when she emerges from her underground lair."

Those weren't Grimluk's exact words. For one thing, Grimluk would never say "dude."

Unfortunately Grimluk wasn't able to sit down and have a nice long chat and explain everything since he could only appear briefly—usually in the reflective chrome surface of a bathroom fixture. So Mack had to operate on very limited information.

The golem that Mack discovered living in Mack's room didn't fill in too many details, either.

A golem, as you may know, is a sort of robot made

of clay. The golem maker writes down an instruction and puts it in the golem's mouth. Then the golem comes alive and does whatever the instruction says.

In the case of the golem in Mack's bedroom, the message said, "Be Mack." So the golem had done its best to look and sound like Mack. He might not be good enough to fool a really close observer, someone who really knew Mack well, but he fooled Mack's parents.

Still, even with a golem, Mack didn't go rushing off to save the world, not right away, because although Mack was open-minded about the whole ancient, smelly, Grimluk-manifestations thing, he wasn't stupid. He needed more information before doing something reckless.

The "more information" came in the form of Paddy "Nine Iron" Trout trying to assassinate Mack by pushing a basketload of highly poisonous snakes into Mack's house. And later, that same Nine Iron tried to run Mack through with a sword while Mack was taking a . . . um . . . utilizing the wall-mounted facilities in the boys' bathroom.

Having escaped the snakes and the sword, Mack

was set upon by two Skirrit, who invaded the school and tried to kill him. Skirrit are one of the evil races that obey the Pale Queen. Think really large grasshoppers walking erect. Grasshoppers or maybe praying mantises, possibly cicadas. Anyway, insectlike and as tall as a short man.

Clearly Richard Gere Middle School needed some new signage. They had a sign forbidding drugs, cigarettes, guns, and alcohol. They had another sign forbidding bikes, skateboards, rollerblades, and scooters. And a third sign forbade iPods, iPhones, and anything else "i." They even had a sign proclaiming the school a nuclear-free zone and a peanut-free zone.

Which was good in case terrorists ever came up with a nuclear peanut.

But there was no sign forbidding Nafia assassins or evil insectoid species in service to the Mother of All Monsters.

Being almost killed by snakes and then chased into a limousine by the Skirrit definitely helped convince Mack to save the world. Plus, in the limousine was an elegant young woman named Rose Everlast, who worked for a very respectable accounting firm. Rose handed Mack and Stefan passports under fake names, and a credit card tied to a million-dollar account.

So, that's where we are. Everything explained.

Except for Princess Ereskigal, known in Greek mythology as Persephone and in Norse mythology as Hel. Not a real popular person, whatever name she used.

Fortunately Mack had used some words of Vargran and turned Risky into burned toast. She was gone. Dead. Vapor. No longer a worry. A ghost. History.

Are you buying that? No?

You're wise to be suspicious. Because Princess Ereskigal is very, very hard to kill.

Four

ABOUT A HUNDRED YEARS AGO, GIVE OR TAKE . . .

You might think that Patrick Trout, the feared Nafia assassin—who would come to be called Paddy and, still later, Nine Iron—would be a product of a bad upbringing.

But no. He was just a rotten kid.

Patrick Joseph Trout was born eighteen seconds after his identical twin, Liam Sean Trout. The birth took place in the back of an oat wagon on the dirt road between the small village of Loathbog and the town of Trollbog.

Within seconds of his birth, Paddy was trying to bite through his twin brother's umbilical cord. Of course Paddy had no teeth—any more than any newborn would—so all he could do was attempt to gum his brother to death, gnawing and crying in a thin newborn wail.

Gnaw gnaw gnaw, waaaah! Gnaw gnaw gnaw, waaaah!

He was a very bad baby.

Both Loathbog and Trollbog were in County Grind. County Grind was known for its beautiful vistas of shockingly green fields, bright pink pigs, and pale amber whiskey.

The reason the Trout family was on its way to Trollbog was to sell their load of oats. No one grew better oats than the Trouts, and Mother Trout was justly renowned for her many oat recipes: oats, oats with salt, oat cereal, oat bread, charred oats, grilled oats, fricasseed oats, barbecued oats, oat kabob, smoked oats, oat fondue, oat pie, oat loaf, oat terrine,

Grimos (like Cheerios but not), oats stuffed with peat, oats à la turf, oats with three types of lichen, oats *sous vide* (she was an early pioneer in the technique), oats with pig feet, oats with pig snout, oats with a reduction of feet and snouts, oat-stuffed pig intestine, oat-stuffed pig stomach, oat-stuffed pig-organ-no-one-knows-the-name-of, oats with whiskey, and of course, oatmeal.

Patrick and Liam were expected to grow up and take over the oat farm. Indeed, they were raised to care about little else. Once Patrick mentioned that some people enjoyed wheat, and his father promptly smacked him with a loaf of oat bread.

Not stale oat bread, because that'll kill you.

By the time he was nine, Patrick could identify all major types of oat blight: oat weevils, oat rust, oat worm, oat mold, false oat mold, and oat-eating falcons.

See, he was trying to be good. Trying not to be just evil. Really, he was.

But as hard as Patrick worked at the science of oats, Liam, as the firstborn, got all the attention from their father. This was because County Grind had a primogeniture law, which meant that the firstborn would inherit everything. The second son was a sort of spare part. A sort of unpaid employee. Only if Liam died would the farm go to Patrick.

But Liam was even healthier than Patrick. So no such luck.

Unless . . .

But murder was frowned on in Loathbog, especially murder of a brother. The punishment was to be drawn and quartered by four powerful horses. Now, since no one could afford horses in Loathbog, they used pigs. And since pigs weren't really strong enough to pull a person apart, it wasn't exactly a death sentence. But it was humiliating, and you could easily dislocate a shoulder.

Cars had just been invented, so there was some thought given to using cars for the drawing and quartering. But seriously, if you can't afford a horse, you sure can't afford a car. I mean, please. Cars in Loathbog? No. It was still pig-drawn wagons in Loathbog. After all, County Grind wasn't exactly County Snoot.

County Snoot: everyone hated those guys.

One day when Patrick was about twelve, his father had a little talk with him. He sat him down on a bale of oats and said, "Um . . . wait, it will come to me . . .

Patrick! Yes, I knew I'd remember your name."

"My friends call me Paddy," he answered tersely.

"You have friends? Ah-ha-ha-ha, that's a good one." Mr. Trout slapped his knee. Patrick's knee. "Sure an' ye have the gift o' blarney, that ye do, that ye do, laddie buck."

I could kill you with a pitchfork, old man is what Patrick did not say, but what he thought.

"Well, I'll get right to it, um . . ."

"Paddy."

"Whatever. As you know, your brother, Liam, is to inherit the farm when your sainted mother 'n' me shuffle off this mortal coil. Now, normally you could stay on and work for Liam."

Patrick produced a sort of low growl mixed with a serpentine hiss.

"But Liam doesn't much like the notion of you hanging around and trying to kill him."

"Me?" Paddy said innocently. "Try to kill him? Me? That's crazy! I'm innocent! Oh, the pain of false accusation!" Then he leaned in close to his father and snarled, "So who told you?"

"The point is, son, we can't have you trying to

murder your brother all the time. We're sending you to America."

"America?"

"For the last nine years your mother has saved all her prize money from the County Grind Fair oat-cooking competitions, and we've now got the money to send you abroad."

"Wait. She's been saving up to get rid of me since I was three years old?"

"No, no, no, laddie. That's just the first time she won any prize money. Lord love ye, we've been trying to get the cost of the ticket set aside since you were four months old and reached for your first meat cleaver. And especially since our farmhand Tommy O'Doul disappeared. By the way, you don't happen to know where Tommy is, do you, laddie?"

"I categorically deny all accusations, and I refuse to answer any questions on the grounds that it may incriminate me," Paddy said.

"Ah, you'll do just fine in America."

Which is how Patrick "Paddy" Trout came to leave Loathbog and County Grind and took ship for the land of opportunity.

Five

Back in Beijing, Stefan and Jarrah took a cab to the brand-new Nine Dragons Hotel.

It was a stunning hotel. Beautiful. Expensive. Swank. All those things. Mack woke up in the elevator, moaning and whining about blue cheese, so as soon as they got to their room, Stefan dragged him to the bathroom, turned the shower on, and tossed him in.

Mack showered using several cleaning agents: hand soap, bath soap, tangerine body wash, and shampoo.

Then he started it all over again. And finally he felt clean of the awful blue-cheesy-guts stuff.

He emerged scrubbed and pink, swathed in a plush bathrobe, and far less likely to whine.

Jarrah had snagged a candy bar from the minifridge and was standing beside Stefan, who was looking out one of the floor-to-ceiling windows.

"You know, you boys didn't mention there was a crazy old loon trying to kill you," Jarrah accused.

"I didn't think he'd come after us," Mack said. He flopped back onto the bed, which was amazingly soft. There were two beds in this room, and another bed in the adjoining room. "I thought Grimluk might have said something about a trap. It wasn't clear. I thought I was imagining it. But I guess that was the trap."

"The possibility of a trap is something you definitely want to mention," Jarrah said. "Still and all, here we are, right as rain. No worries."

Jarrah was a cheerful, optimistic sort of girl. Mack wished he could be like that. The cheerful, optimistic part, not the girl part.

Stefan was looking at the room service menu. "I can't read this."

Jarrah took the menu from him, flipped from

the Chinese-language pages to the English-language pages, and handed it back.

"Huh," Stefan said.

"That was weird, wasn't it?" Jarrah said thoughtfully. "I mean, so I say these Vargran words, and stuff happens. I mean, that's weird, right?"

Mack lifted his head. "Some people might think so. Like, sane people. They would think so."

Jarrah took a thoughtful bite of her candy bar. "I mean, what's weird is that I'd spoken Vargran before. While I was with me mum and she was working on the Uluru cave wall. We'd puzzle words out. But nothing ever happened before. Not like that. Not something supernatural."

Stefan said, "It's all Chinese food. Except the club sandwich." He tossed the menu aside and turned on the TV.

"I think there's some kind of match-up between the person and the things they can do with Vargran," Mack said. "I don't know. I tried Google, Bing, Wolfram|Alpha, all the search engines. There isn't much about Vargran."

"You think they'll eventually shrink back? The Lepercons, I mean?"

This Book is about Mack, not about me. I'm just his Golem. So you don't have to read this part. Unless you want to. Do you want to? Are you holding the book sideways so you can read it? Are people staring at you because you're reading a book sideways? Do you feel kind kind of silly? I feel silly a lot. Like the other day when it rained and my feet got wet and started dissolving. I was running late, so no time to stop and re-mud myself. By the time I got to class, I was missing all my knees. I felt silly. Also short. Then kids started screaming.

Mack nodded at the TV, which was showing a news report. It was an exterior shot of the airport. There were police cars and ambulances with lights flashing.

A small army of workers pushed wheelbarrows full of goo that looked a bit like soft blue cheese. Firefighters had hooked up a hose and were spraying down some very disgruntled-looking people and their luggage.

The broadcast was in Mandarin—one of the two main Chinese languages—so no one understood the commentary. But Mack guessed it was something like, "Holy fajita, the airport baggage claim is full of giant creatures oozing stinky cheese. What the heck is going on?"

"This Vargran stuff is cool," Stefan said. "I could buy a Snickers, right? And Jarrah, you could do your magico mumbo jabumbo and make it, like, huge."

"And then we'd be smothered in creamy nougat," Mack pointed out.

"Nah. Just eat your way out," Stefan said. He made a face like he thought maybe Mack was being an idiot.

"I don't know what we're supposed to do," Mack said. He got up and went to stand between Stefan and Jarrah at the window. They were on the twenty-first floor, high up. It was dusk; lights were just coming on all over the city.

"We have thirty-five days," Mack said. "We have to find ten more kids. The exactly right ten more kids. We can't just go to the nearest middle school. Then we have to, like . . . Well, I don't exactly know. Grimluk said we had to find these ancient, unknown forces. And mostly, we had to learn Vargran."

"Well, my mum is working on deciphering more of that," Jarrah said. "Why did Grimluk send us here to China?"

"All Grimluk told me was, go to the nine dragons of Daidu. If I hadn't Googled it, I wouldn't even have known Daidu was the ancient name for Beijing. There was only one hotel named the Nine Dragons Hotel. So. Here we are."

"We're here to find the next one of our group, right?" Jarrah said. "So, it's what, like a billion people in China? No worries, we just start asking around."

"Let's go out and get some food," Stefan said.

"We only have thirty-five days!" Mack cried.

"We still have to eat," Jarrah said. "And we're here, right? Let's go out, see what's what. Maybe the third member of the Magnificent Twelve is at the local McDonald's."

"It's getting dark," Mack said, but it was a weak objection because Stefan and Jarrah were already on their way.

The hotel was situated on a broad avenue. Traffic wasn't heavy but it was dangerous. There were more bikes than buses, more buses than taxis, more taxis than private cars. But none of them seemed overly concerned with traffic lights.

The Magnificent Two plus Stefan had a map, given to them at the hotel. Marked on it was the night market, the Donghuamen.

Seriously. That's the actual name.

The woman at the hotel had told them it was the place to go for food. They could see the bright glow of it from blocks away.

"It's right next to the Forbidden City," Mack said, turning the map in his hands.

"Forbidden," Stefan said with a smirk. "Yeah, well, it's not forbidden to me."

Jarrah laughed. "Got that right, mate."

(Author's note: I forgot to mention that Mack had changed out of his bathrobe. So if you were picturing him still in a robe, no: regular clothes.)

Mack read the brief description on the map. "The

Forbidden City is open to anyone nowadays. It's this gigantic palace complex. Bunch of palaces and museums and stuff, with nine thousand nine hundred ninety-nine rooms. Back in the old days no man could enter. Instant death. Unless you were a eunuch."

"What's a eunuch?" Stefan asked.

Mack told him, and as a result Stefan headed into the Donghuamen Night Market walking a little strangely.

The market was about four dozen blazingly bright stalls topped by cheery red-striped awnings. The attendants all wore red caps and red aprons and screeched insistently at the passing crowd. It was very clean and well-organized, and smelled of fresh fish.

The food choices were rather unusual. First, most of the food was on sticks. Like shish kebab. Or corn dogs. Except that these were no corn dogs.

There were fried silkworm cocoons on a stick.

Fried grasshoppers on a stick.

Fried beetles on a stick.

Seriously, none of these are made up.

Fried sea horse on a stick.

Fried starfish on a stick.

Fried scorpion on a stick.

And fried snake wrapped around a stick.

The philosophy at Donghuamen seemed to be: Is it really gross? Okay then, put it on a stick!

The crowd was predominantly Chinese, and mostly they weren't eating the various stick-based foods. They were eating little buns stuffed with meat and vegetables, or pointing at pieces of fish and having it fried up in blistering-hot woks. Or chewing brightly colored glazed fruit.

It was the American, British, and Australian tourists eating the OMG-on-a-stick food.

"Huh. Those are, like, bugs," Stefan said. "Bugs on a stick."

"You're not scared to try them, are you?" Mack taunted.

Stefan narrowed his eyes, shot a dirty look at Mack, but then noticed Jarrah smiling expectantly at him.

"I will if you will," Jarrah said. She had a dazzling smile. At least Stefan looked dazzled by it.

"Yeah?"

Mack rolled his eyes. "You guys really don't have to."

"Starfish?" Jarrah suggested.

"Why, you scared to eat a fried snake?"

"Oh, I'll eat a fried snake, mate," Jarrah shot back. "The question is, are you man enough to eat a fried silkworm cocoon?"

It was a strange sort of courting ritual, Mack decided. Two crazy people sizing each other up.

"Scorpion," Stefan said.

Jarrah high-fived him. "You're on."

They bought two orders of scorpion on a stick. Each stick had three small scorpions.

Stefan said, "Okay, at the same—"

Jarrah didn't wait. She chewed one of the scorpions, and Stefan had to rush to keep up.

"The two of you are mental," Mack said as Jarrah and Stefan laughed and crunched away with scorpion tails sticking out of their mouths.

"Oh, come on, don't be a wimp, Mack," Jarrah teased. "At least try a fried grasshopper. They don't look so bad."

Mack made a face and looked dubiously at the plastic tray loaded with fried grasshoppers. "Yeah, I don't think so. They look a little bit too much like those . . ."

The words died in his mouth. What the grasshoppers looked like were Skirrit.

One of which, wearing a tan trench coat and a narrow-brimmed fedora that didn't exactly hide his giant bug head, had just stepped up beside Mack.

Six

"**S**kirrrrrriiiiiittt!" Mack yelled.

He jerked away from the food, away from the Skirrit in the trench coat. But another was right behind him and wrapped its insect stick arms around him. The first pulled a bladed weapon like a short, curved sword from beneath its coat and pointed it at Mack's chest.

A ripple went through the crowd of tourists as more and more realized that a couple of very big grasshoppers—grasshoppers not unlike the ones some of them were eating—were kidnapping a kid.

People ran. The vendors and cooks working the food stands ran. It took about four seconds for everyone to go from normal to complete panic, and then it was screaming and running and knocking over hot woks, and awning poles broken and ice bins spilled all over the sidewalk, and everywhere food: food flying and food dropping and food slithering because it was still alive.

A giant glass aquarium full of octopi shattered, and hundreds of confused octopi attached their suckers to legs and sandaled feet and bicycle tires.

That last part was actually kind of funny. If you ever get the chance, attach an octopus to a bicycle tire and ride around. You'll see.

Then the first flames appeared as hot wok met spilled oil.

"Back off, bugs!" Stefan roared.

He threw himself, fists pummeling, at the Skirrit that held Mack tight.

"He's got a . . ." Mack had wanted to yell, *He's got a knife*; but it wasn't exactly a knife and Mack didn't know quite what it was, so he ended up just yelling, "He's got a" followed by ellipses.

But Stefan had seen the blade. With sheer, brute force he lifted the Skirrit and Mack together in one armload, spun around, and slammed the first Skirrit straight into the outthrust blade of the second.

"Ayahgaaah!" the stabbed Skirrit cried.

His grip on Mack loosened. And loosened still more when Jarrah snatched up one of the confused octopi and hurled it into the Skirrit's face.

"Thanks," Mack gasped.

But thanks were premature. There was still one Skirrit left.

He advanced on Mack with his nameless blade out and ready. "You die," the Skirrit said. With blinding speed he switched the blade from one hand to the other and lunged. The blade hit—*shunk!*—a plastic tray held up as a shield by Stefan.

The blade went right through the plastic tray but stuck. Stefan twisted the tray, trying to yank the blade from the bug's hand.

And . . . yeah, that didn't work.

Instead the Skirrit pulled the blade free, took a

step back to steady himself, stepped on the ice that had been spilled, did a comic little cartoon wobble, and landed on his face, hard.

Stefan was on him fast. He stomped on the bug's blade and with his other foot crushed the exoskeletal arm.

"Ayahgaaaaaahh!" the Skirrit cried.

Apparently that is the Skirrit cry of pain.

Stefan picked up the blade, smiled, and began to admire the weapon. Jarrah looked on, admiring both Stefan and the blade.

There came the sound of sirens approaching. At least one of the food stands was burning. Its red-and-white-striped awning sent flames shooting high into the night sky.

The crowd had backed away to a distance and were each and every one fumbling with cell phones to take pictures and video.

"I don't want to be a YouTube sensation twice in one day," Mack said. "Let's get out of here."

They turned their backs on the chaotic, burning, but still somehow cheerful market, and plunged through the crowds that were now rushing to see what all the yelling was about.

They practically stumbled into a mass of people on bicycles.

Short people on bicycles.

So short, especially in their stumpy legs, that they'd each strapped wooden blocks to their feet so they could reach the pedals.

Mack was just noticing this odd fact when he was smacked on the side of the head by a club shaped a bit like a bowling pin.

Tong Elves, he thought dreamily as his legs turned to jelly and he circled the drain of consciousness.

That's right: circled the drain of consciousness. You have a problem with that?

Mack barely avoided being completely flushed out of consciousness. He sank to his knees, and Jarrah hauled him back up.

The mob of Tong Elves on bikes shot past, braked, turned clumsily back, and came in a rush for a second pass.

"You got a magic spell for this?" Stefan asked.

"I miss Toaster Strudel," Mack said.

Stefan and Jarrah correctly interpreted this remark

as evidence that the blow to Mack's head might have scattered his wits a bit.

"Run!" Stefan said to Jarrah.

"Got that right!" Jarrah agreed.

They each grabbed one of Mack's arms and took off, half guiding, half dragging Mack, who was explaining why strawberry Toaster Strudel was the best, but sometimes he liked the apple.

"I had a s'mores flavor Toaster Strudel once but . . . ," Mack announced before losing his train of thought.

The Tong Elves were just a few feet away. But they were awkward on their bikes. Stefan led Mack and Jarrah straight across their path, rushed into traffic, and dodged across the street through buses and taxis.

The Tong Elves veered to follow.

Wham! A bus reduced their number by two. The unlucky pair went flying through the air and landed in front of a taxi, which hit them again—*wham!*—and flipped them bike-over-heels into a light pole.

"I like foosball," Mack said. "But I'm not good at it."

"This way! We can't outrun them on foot!" Stefan yelled, and he and Jarrah dragged Mack bouncing and scuffling down the sidewalk and into a rack of parked bicycles. The bikes were locked, but Stefan still had the Skirrit blade.

Thwack! Thwack! Thwack!

And there were three unlocked bikes.

"Can you ride a bike?" Jarrah asked Mack.

Mack drew himself up with offended dignity and said, "I could be a Jonas brother."

"I think that's a no," Jarrah said.

Stefan lifted Mack up and settled him on the handlebars of a bike. With fluid strength Stefan swung a leg over, mounted the bike, held a drifting, ranting Mack in place with one hand, grabbed the handlebar with the other, and stomped on the pedal.

Down the street, past the now partly flame-engulfed market they rode, with a mob of Tong Elves on bikes behind them.

But then, just ahead, a pedicab.

Small digression: a pedicab is defined on wordia.com as "noun, a pedal-operated tricycle, available for hire, with an attached seat for one or two passengers."

This particular pedicab had a wiry guy pedaling.

And on the back it had a sort of cabin, bright turquoise with a red fringe and gold tassels.

The pedicab was speeding right toward Mack and Stefan. As fast as the guy could pedal.

And leaning out of the side of the cabin, with the naked blade of his cane-sword pointed forward like a knight with a jousting lance, was Paddy "Nine Iron" Trout.

Seven

ABOUT NINETY YEARS AGO, GIVE OR TAKE . . .

"So long, son!" Paddy's parents shouted as they waved to him from the quay. "We'll . . ." They paused and looked at each other, each hoping the other would say, "We'll miss you."

But in the end neither could quite pull it off. So they just repeated, "So long!"

Paddy shipped out for America aboard HMS

DiCaprio, a luxury transatlantic ship. At least it was luxury if you were in first class. But the *DiCaprio* had seven different classes of accommodation.

In first class you lived like a king. A giant stateroom, a butler, a maid, two bathrooms, crystal chandeliers, gold doorknobs, lovely soft feather beds. The toilet paper was linen, and the linens were silk. In the bathroom there were three knobs: hot, cold, and soup. The food served was so fresh you could actually meet the chickens who laid your eggs and the pigs who would become your bacon.

But none of that mattered because Paddy was not in first class.

In second class you were still doing pretty well, with a nice little stateroom. There was no soup nozzle in the room, and the toilet paper was just paper, but it was soft (two-ply). And second-class passengers were served pleasant and healthy meals in the cheerful second-class dining room. You didn't get to actually chat with your pig or lamb or chicken or cow, but you could wave to them.

But Paddy was not in second class.

Third class was a little more rough-and-ready. You

had to make your own bed, for one thing. And meals were all self-serve at the oat 'n' swine buffet.

Nope, not third class, either.

Fourth class was where most impoverished emigrants traveled. They cooked their own meals over open fires in massively overcrowded holds down in the sweaty bowels of the ship, where they dreamed of spotting the Statue of Liberty.

Paddy was not in fourth class.

Fifth-class passengers weren't even given a place to spread out a blanket. Mostly they climbed into laundry bags and hung those bags from hooks. Thus they rocked back and forth all night, banging up against the steel bulkheads with each passing wave. They were kept awake by the mystery of how they could hang up a bag they were actually in. Their meals were served at the same time as the livestock kept for the first-class passengers' dinners were fed. In fact, it was the same food.

Fifth class didn't dream of spotting the Statue of Liberty because if they ever appeared on the open deck, they'd get a beat-down from beefy ship's stewards. The only time they were allowed on deck was for gladiatorial games in which they were pitted against each other in pepper mill battles while first-class

So, MAYBE I SHOULD EXPLAIN BECAUSE YOU MAY NOT KNOW VERY MUCH ABOUT GOLEMS. FIRST OF ALL, IT'S GOLEM, LIKE GO AND THEN LEM. NOT GOLLUM. I AM NOT GOLLUM. I DON'T WANTS IT, PRECIOUS. A GOLLUM IS 90 PERCENT HOBBIT AND 10 PERCENT EVIL. A GOLEM IS 90 PERCENT MUD, AND ANOTHER 7 PERCENT TWIGS, PINECONES, DEAD BEETLES, AND LINT. THE LAST 3 PERCENT IS FAITHFULNESS. WE ARE VERY FAITHFUL. I WILL ALWAYS FAITHFULLY TRY TO TAKE MACK'S PLACE WHILE HE'S AWAY. EVEN THOUGH IT MEANS I HAVE DETENTION BECAUSE OF THE WHOLE DISSOLVED-FEET SITUATION AND THE SCREAMING AND ALL.

passengers bet on the outcome.

Fifth class? Tough place. Unpleasant place.

But Paddy was not in fifth class. He'd have loved to be fifth class.

Sixth class meant you slept in the fifth-class bathrooms, or heads as they say on boats. You could sit on one of the toilets until someone needed to use it. This wasn't a great way to spend ten days, which was how long it took the HMS *DiCaprio* to get across the ocean to New York.

But Paddy wasn't in sixth class.

Paddy was in seventh class. And seventh class was a very bad class aboard the *DiCaprio*. Seventh-class passengers were allowed aboard the ship, but once aboard they were hunted by the packs of wild dogs that lived down in the bilges.

The wild dogs were the offspring of escaped pets. You see, sometimes first-class passengers traveled with poodles or Chihuahuas or Pekingese. Over the years some of these animals had escaped their kennels and had bred and multiplied in the bowels of the great ship.

Imagine, if you will, poodles bred with Chihuahuas and then hardened and made savage by the dog pack life in the dank, dark holds far, far from light.

Nobody would want to go up against that kind of horror.

The bilges of a ship are the lowest level. Down below the engines. Not even the basement of the ship, more like if the ship had a basement but someone dug out a pit below that.

Anyway, the bilges were where all the water that seeped into the ship collected. Rainwater, sea spray, mop water, overflowing toilet water, spilled coffee water, seasickness results, you name it. It was about up to Paddy's thighs. It smelled like a toilet.

For food, the seventh-class passengers had to trap and kill one of the many alligators that slithered through the dank, cold, oily, poo-smelling water.

So basically it was bad. Very bad. As bad as flying coach out of O'Hare.

But Paddy was a tough kid. On his first night in the bilges he earned the respect of the wild dog pack by biting the pack's leader on the ear and gnawing away for so long that forever after that dog was known as Rex "One Ear" Plantagenet.

On his second night Paddy killed and ate an alligator.

By the time he left the *DiCaprio*—seventh-class passengers didn't walk down the gangplank; they were tossed into the water and left to swim ashore—he not only had a belly full of tasty alligator sushi, he had a nice pair of homemade alligator boots and a matching alligator vest.

Which was frankly disturbing to the first New Yorkers who saw him, what with Paddy having had no facilities for drying or even properly cleaning alligator skin. So his alligator boots had bits of alligator intestine trailing behind.

On the plus side, no one asked him for spare change.

Paddy went straight from the dock to the headquarters of the Toomany Society, which was housed in Toomany Hall. The Toomany Society offered help to newly arrived immigrants.

"What do you do for a living?" the woman at the desk asked.

"I used to grow oats."

"That'll be really useful here in New York. We have so many vast fields of oats."

"Are you being sarcastic?" Paddy asked.

"Actually, no. I mean, this isn't New York like it might be in the future, say, the far-off twenty-first century. This is New York in the early twentieth century. And believe it or not, we still have farms here. A hardworking oater can eke out a miserable existence working sixteen backbreaking hours a day, seven days a week in harsh conditions. You'll marry a dance hall girl, spawn ill-mannered brats, grow old before your time, and die of some miserable disease, possibly consumption. But hey, it's a living."

"What are my other choices?" Paddy asked.

The woman shrugged. "You're not fit for anything but oat farming or banking—and you don't have the wardrobe for banking. And then, there's always crime."

"Tell me about this 'crime' of which you speak."

"Well, hmm . . . I suppose you'd join a criminal gang, extort money from shopkeepers, rob banks, dress in flashy clothes, and mostly sit around all day drinking with other criminals in between acts of mayhem."

Paddy pointed a jaunty finger at her and said, "Bingo."

Eight

"**M**y favorite color used to be purple!" Mack cried out as Stefan and Jarrah pedaled frantically.

The Tong Elves were just behind them.

Nine Iron Trout was just ahead, ready to impale them.

Clearly the Pale Queen's minions weren't waiting around for the thirty-five days to be up. They were looking for a quick kill.

Or in Nine Iron's case, a slow kill.

Panicky vendors were trying desperately to save squids and snakes-on-a-stick from the threatening flames. All the commotion was lit by cheery neon lights shining off candy-striped awnings.

Stefan had powerful legs. But the weight of a not-exactly-steady Mack flailing all over the handlebars slowed him down a bit.

Mack didn't snap entirely back to reality until he saw Nine Iron's cane-sword within about eight feet of skewering him like a fried scorpion.

"Hey!" he yelled.

Stefan tried to veer right to pass the safe side of the pedicab, but quick-peddling Tong Elves cut him off.

"Left! Closer!" Mack shouted.

Maybe Stefan obeyed or maybe he just wobbled, but either way Mack's left hand came just close enough to a tray of mixed skewers.

He snatched them up, transferred them to his right hand, and with Nine Iron's deadly sword just two feet from his heart, flung the skewers like darts.

The sudden movement sent Stefan even farther left, crashing through a grease fire and slip-sliding through a couple of dozen frantic lobsters who were no doubt hoping to reach the ocean. (Sorry: no.)

The sword missed by millimeters.

The skewers did not. In a flash of neon, Mack saw that a skewer of fried sea horses had stuck in Nine Iron's gaunt cheek. And a skewer of fried silkworm cocoons had stuck in Nine Iron's green bowler hat.

They flashed past the pedicab and gained speed. Jarrah was alongside, pedaling hard.

"Why am I riding on the handlebars?" Mack cried.

"Look out! Here they come!" Jarrah cried, jerking her chin back toward the Tong Elves. With a glance, Mack could see that the pedicab driver had spun his vehicle sharply, making a teetering two-wheel turn, and now raced after the fleeing bikes.

Ahead was a tall, red-lacquered double door studded with brass bolts as big as a baby's head. Two uniformed guards were just closing a massive filigreed gate behind a departing cleaning crew.

Mack, Stefan, and Jarrah shot through the gap, pursued by Chinese shouts of outrage. Which aren't that different from American shouts of outrage because outrage is a universal language.

The guards slammed the gates closed behind them, locking out Nine Iron and the elves on bikes.

Unfortunately now the guards were yelling at Mack, Stefan, and Jarrah, and blowing police whistles, so while things looked better than they had, they still didn't look good.

"We have to hide!" Jarrah said.

They were in a vast square. Buildings all around formed the edges of a cobblestoned courtyard. The walls on all sides were reddish, although in the dim light it was hard to see very clearly.

Mack was trying to picture the map of the Forbidden City in his mind. He'd glanced at the map but he hadn't exactly memorized the place. After all, it's a huge complex full of numerous palaces—some big, some small, all fabulously decorated with dragons and filigree and Chinese characters.

And still, even now, Mack was thinking just a little bit about Toaster Strudel.

"Which way?" Stefan asked.

They were easily outpacing the guards, who were on foot. But Mack had no illusion that these were the only guards. In a few minutes the place would be swarming with guards and cops and, for all he knew, the entire Chinese army.

Things had loosened up a bit at the Forbidden City, but not so much that they'd let two Yanks and an Aussie ride bikes around the place at night.

"Just keep riding!" Mack yelled.

They were pedaling up a long ramp that led to one of the central palaces.

"If there's ten thousand rooms," Jarrah said, "we should be able to find someplace to hide."

"Nine thousand nine hundred ninety-nine rooms," Mack corrected her. "The palace of the gods was ten thousand, and emperors didn't want to look presumptuous by equaling it."

Jarrah stared at him. Mack shrugged. "What? I notice these things."

"We have to ditch the bikes," Jarrah said. "We can hide easier on foot."

They ducked inside through one of the less grandiose entrances. The lights had been turned off, but emergency exits still glowed and a single distant overhead light shone. They saw a museum, a square chamber filled with ornate clocks and other bits of furniture, which on closer examination also turned out to be clocks.

"Clock museum," Mack whispered. He had his iPhone out and was frantically web surfing, trying to pull up a map of the Forbidden City.

"Cool," Jarrah said. "The kind of place Mum would love."

Stefan backed into a massive, incredibly fragile-looking clock that rocked back on its pedestal.

Mack heard the sound of running footsteps.

He dimmed the screen on his phone.

"This way," Jarrah said. "Shine a little phone light on this."

It was a cabinet at the bottom of an armoire-sized clock decorated with elephants and griffins and little gold leaves. The clock was maybe nine feet tall. But the cabinet wasn't much bigger than a large toy box.

"We could hide in there," Stefan said. "The guards are closing in on this place."

"Are you nuts?" Mack whispered back. "I'm not getting in there! It's tiny! We could be locked in there forever. No air. Suffocating! I won't be able to breathe. . . . Already I can't breathe. . . . Like being buried alive! I can't!"

Running footsteps were approaching. Flashlight beams cast skittery pools of light by the nearest entryway.

"Dude!" Stefan hissed. "Where did the Tong Elves hit you?"

Mack pointed to his left temple. So Stefan hit him in his right temple.

It was a while before Mack regained consciousness.

It was a while longer before he realized he had his head in Stefan's armpit. And Jarrah's head between his ankles.

Then it really hit him.

Mack opened his mouth to scream, but Stefan's hand was clasped firmly over it, so all he could do was yell, "Mmmm! Mmmmm! Mph-puh-rrrnnn!"

"I think the coast is clear," Jarrah said.

"Mmmm mmmm hhhrrggh!" Mack shouted as Stefan and Jarrah unpacked themselves.

"I'm going to take my hand away, Mack," Stefan said. "No screaming, okay?"

Stefan released Mack, who sucked air for several

minutes, like Nine Iron Trout after a marathon.

"Sorry," Mack said. "I realize I'm nuts. Okay? I know it's craziness."

Jarrah patted him on the back. "No worries, mate; we're all nuts or we wouldn't be here, would we?" Then, more serious, she said, "I felt something in there. Something carved inside the cabinet. Give us the phone light for a minute." She aimed his phone light into the cabinet. "Yeah. You can't see it; it's carved in bas-relief."

She fumbled for Mack's hand and pressed it against the carving. Mack felt intricate bumps and swirls.

"It's decoration," he hissed.

"Nah. I don't think so. It was squashed into me bum for the better part of half an hour."

Mack focused and ran his fingers carefully, delicately over the carved area. "It's like letters."

Jarrah looked over Mack's shoulder, then reached past him to feel the letters. "I think it's Vargran. It has the same letters."

"Can you read it?"

"Not all of it. Just a bit. Feel that? That's the number nine. Nine snakes? Nine snakes on a wall?"

"I saw that movie. Awesome!" Stefan said.

Mack listened hard. No more footsteps. The guards had definitely gone on to search the other 9,998 rooms.

"Yeah, that's Vargran," Jarrah said. "Nine hidden snakes. I think. And then a math problem."

"A what?"

"A math problem: what is three fours?"

"Eight?" Stefan guessed. Then, in the embarrassed silence, "I'm not that good at math."

"Twelve," Jarrah said. She squeezed Stefan's arm, comforting. "You're good at other things."

"How do we get out of here, that's the question," Mack said.

He turned reluctantly from the clock cabinet and stood up, sore knees cracking. Just in time to see Nine Iron thrust with his cane-sword.

Stefan saw it a split second sooner and was a split second quicker to react. He jumped in front of Mack. The blade pierced Stefan in the center of his chest.

Stefan cried out in surprise and pain.

Jarrah rushed at Nine Iron and shoved him onto his butt. The sword went flying, twirling across the polished tile floor.

Mack caught Stefan as he slumped forward.

"Dude!" Mack cried.

"Huh," Stefan remarked. He put a hand over the hole. Blood seeped through his fingers.

Mack heard shouts and rushing feet. No way to know whether it was guards or elves, and it probably didn't matter.

"Run!" Mack hissed.

They ran, with Stefan moving at half speed and looking as if he'd soon be going slower.

Much slower.

Nine

"**R**un!"

They ran. Out into the courtyard. Dozens of flashlights stabbed the darkness like light sabers. Chinese voices were yelling.

Mack didn't know what they were yelling, but it was probably "Get them!"

They passed beneath an arch, up a ramp, down a staircase, running blind, no idea where they were going, just running.

But as they ran, Mack kept thinking he really should stop, give himself up. The guards would call an ambulance for Stefan. They could probably save his life.

But if they gave up, Mack would be kicked out of the country and sent home. What would become of the Magnificent Twelve then?

This was not the kind of decision Mack liked to make. Doom Stefan or doom the world. That wasn't like choosing between shorts and jeans. This was life and death.

But it probably wasn't going to matter much. Because suddenly Mack, Jarrah, and Stefan had run out of places to run.

They were boxed in. Guards were closing from three directions, and the fourth direction was a wall beautifully decorated in tile. Ten flashlights were in their faces, blinding their eyes.

"We have to give up," Mack said to Jarrah.

Mack's phone rang. He jumped about three feet in the air. "Aaah!"

"Two . . . three . . . seven . . . nine!" Jarrah said.

"What are you counting?" Mack pulled out his phone. The display showed his home number. No way

TODAY MACK'S TEACHER SAID, "WHERE IS YOUR ENGLISH PAPER, MR. MACAVOY?" I SAID, "IN ENGLAND?" THE TEACHER SENT ME A VERY HARD LOOK. "YOUR ENGLISH PAPER, MR. MACAVOY. THE ONE I ASSIGNED LAST WEEK." THIS WAS CONFUSING, SO I SAID, "I DON'T UNDERSTAND ASS SIGN." SO NOW I HAVE EXTRA DETENTION. DOUBLE DETAINED. I THINK I HAD BETTER CALL MACK ABOUT THE ENGLISH PAPER. I HOPE HE'S NOT BUSY.

he could answer it, no way.

"The wall! Look at it!"

Mack turned away from the advancing guards. The decorated wall wasn't just pretty tile. Jarrah was right: nine brightly colored dragons cavorted down the hundred-foot length of it.

"Huh," Stefan said, but he wasn't appreciating the wall. He was noticing that some small shadows were creeping up behind the guards, even as the guards were edging closer.

"Back off, you quivering jelly bags of mucus!" one of the Tong Elves said. "They're ours!"

It's possible the guards understood them. But it's more likely they were just startled to see that they were surrounded.

By elves in lederhosen.

That would startle most people.

"What?" Mack yelled into the phone. "Who is it? I'm kind of busy!"

"Hi, Mack! It's me, your golem!"

"What?" Mack shrieked.

"I'm looking for the English paper. Do you know where you might have put it? It's already late, and our teacher—"

"What? *What?*"

"The English paper—"

"I'm kind of busy right now!" Mack screamed. "It's in my laptop. The folder marked 'Useless Stuff.'"

"Thanks! Bye-bye, real Mack."

The flashlights all swung around to highlight the new threat. Probably seventeen or eighteen—Mack wasn't really concerned with counting—Tong Elves, each armed with a chubby billy club, formed a menacing semicircle.

"The walking human slime are ours," the elf leader snarled. "So step aside in the name of the Pale Queen, you sock puppets stuffed with pig filth!"

One of the guards evidently understood this well enough. He translated for his comrades. Suddenly the guards—who had been pretty determined to catch Mack and his friends—found a whole different motivation.

The guards wore green uniforms with white belts that went around their waists and over their right shoulders. They had brass buttons and red epaulets, and the only weapons they had were their flashlights. Mack was pretty sure he was going to witness an elf-on-guard massacre.

But then one of the guards shouted an order. Moving as one, the guards holstered their flashlights, laid their hats carefully aside on the cobblestones, and adopted martial arts stances.

"Kee-*yah*!"

The guards leaped!

The Tong Elves rushed!

It was kung fu fists versus Tong Elf clubs.

"Cool. They should totally make a game of this," Stefan said. Then, "Owww. My chest kind of hurts."

"The nine dragons in Beijing," Jarrah shouted, to be heard over the sounds of kicks and grunts and kung fu punches. "It wasn't the hotel. It was this wall!"

"Yeah," Mack agreed. "But when this fight's over, we won't be either place."

Jarrah stared with amazing concentration, totally ignoring the fight that raged behind her.

"The Magnificent Twelve," she said.

"Not yet we're not," Mack said.

"In Vargran. 'The Magnificent Twelve' in Vargran! I remember seeing this at Uluru. It was one of the keys to deciphering the whole alphabet." And then, she said it. Aloud. In Vargran.

"*Eb Magga Ull-tway.*"

And then! Nothing!

"That didn't work," Jarrah said, sounding a bit surprised. "You try it, Mack."

So Mack said, "*Eb Magga Ull-tway!*"

The wall, all one hundred by ten feet of it, tilted back and then slid straight down into the ground with a slight grinding noise.

A wide, dark staircase led into the earth.

"Oh, fine, it works for you." Jarrah pouted. "Go or no go?"

Mack hesitated. If he kept going and didn't get Stefan to a doctor immediately, Stefan might bleed to death.

Stefan had become a friend. That realization came as a shock to Mack. In the space of just a few days, really, Stefan had gone from bully to protector. Mack had realized that part, the bodyguard thing. But until this moment he hadn't really noticed that he actually liked Stefan.

Stefan had been hurt protecting Mack. That had to count for a lot.

But the fate of the world might rest on this decision. And the single word *trap* was definitely bouncing around inside his head like a Ping-Pong ball with attention-deficit/hyperactivity disorder.

Sure, Ping-Pong balls can have ADHD. Absolutely.

But this wasn't the time for Mack to contemplate the problems of Ping-Pong balls. This was decision time.

Stefan was a friend. But he was a friend who would want Mack to save the world.

Mack tightened his supporting grip around Stefan. And he stepped across the threshold into an unimagined realm.

Ten

ABOUT NINETY YEARS AGO, MORE OR LESS . . .

After landing in America, Paddy Soon-to-be-Nine-Iron Trout had gone to the Toomany Society for some guidance and had learned that his best career option was crime.

The Toomany Society lady sent him to an address north of Wall Street, where all the best criminal organizations had offices. It was a place they called Five Points Hall.

Five Points Hall was a large, cavernous space built around a huge enclosed courtyard. In that courtyard were various booths, each with pamphlets and literature set out. Paddy walked wonderingly past the Wounded Chickens Gang booth with its promises of drinking, carousing, street fighting, and extortion; past the Black Hand booth, which focused more on exotic foods redolent of garlic and which offered a career in crime regardless of how fat you got; and the Kosher Nostra, where he stopped and spoke with their recruiter.

He learned that the Kosher Nostra engaged in every manner of crime except for the mixing of dairy products with beef.

"But afterward, we feel bad," the Kosher Nostra recruiter said with a shrug.

"After you mix beef and dairy?"

"After we do crimes. These other schmendricks"— he gestured toward the Wounded Chickens and the Black Hand—"they do whatever, then they have a cannelloni or drink a bottle of whiskey. But us, we feel guilty." He held out a plate of pastry. "Would you like a rugelach? Apricot. They're to die for."

Paddy decided this wasn't quite the right criminal organization for him. Then he spotted the smallest of the booths. It was hardly a booth, in fact, just a card table manned by a sullen, furious-faced man in a too-large striped suit. The man was playing solitaire with a dirty, bent-up deck of cards. On the table was a half-finished bowl of something Paddy recognized: oatmeal.

"Aren't you going to finish that?" Paddy asked boldly.

The furious-faced man looked up at him. Furiously. A sneer distorted his face, which was further distorted by what had to be a knife scar running from the corner of his left eye to his right jaw.

"No," the man spat angrily. "It lacks any real appeal. Altogether a bland, unimaginative dish."

"Try toasting some pecans," Paddy said. "Toasted pecans, and instead of milk maybe a dollop of crème fraîche. Clover honey would sweeten it nicely."

The man squinted at Paddy. "You're not married, are you?"

"No."

"Have a girlfriend?"

"No."

"Good. Crime is a great life. But it's not for a family man. It's a lonely life, kid. A life of violence and money and flashy clothes and money and then some more violence."

"I tried to kill my own twin brother."

"Nice." The furious-faced man nodded thoughtfully. "Just the kind of ruthless, amoral, psychopathic young fellow we're looking for." He put down his deck of cards and reached inside his jacket. He whipped out a business card.

The card had the single word *Scarnose*. And an address.

"You're Scarnose?" Paddy asked.

The man looked a bit sheepish. "I wanted *Scarface*. But it was taken." He looked Paddy up and down. "So, you want a life of crime. Do you have any objection to serving the murderous Mother of All Monsters, who is plotting her distant return, at which time she will enslave the entire human race?"

"Meh," Paddy said.

"Go to the address on the card."

"I'll do that," Paddy said. "Say, what's the name of this gang?"

Scarnose grinned (insofar as he was capable of grinning) and said, "You've just signed up with the Nafia, kid."

The Nafia had a very rigid system of promotion. Young Paddy started out as an "eel." An eel spent his days running errands and occasionally attending classes in criminal culture and technique.

(Incidentally, criminal-culture-and-technique school was quite strict. Fail one test, and you were put on horse-poop pickup detail. Fail a second test, and the teacher would hurl you out of a second-floor window. Fail a third test, and the teacher could remove one of your eyeballs and make you eat it. This was not exactly Montessori.)

Paddy enjoyed the life of an eel. But one day an older kid shoved him out of the way, and Paddy beat the boy severely with a fruitcake (a fresh fruitcake fortunately, or it would have been murder).

At which point Paddy was promoted to "miscreant."

Miscreants still had to run errands and attend the occasional class, but they were also given real duties, mostly as lookouts.

Once while acting as a lookout, Paddy was approached by a suspicious police officer. Paddy shoved the police officer. At which point the cop delivered a beat-down with his billy club.

Naturally Paddy was promoted from miscreant to "malefactor."

A malefactor did not run errands or attend classes but acted as a sort of freelance criminal, responsible for shoplifting, purse-cutting, and the snatching of men's pocket watches. (Ninety years ago, remember? They weren't stealing iPods.)

Paddy proved to be quite good at his work. He was a malefactor until the age of sixteen, when he was promoted to "thug."

It was a proud moment because Paddy was the youngest person ever to be so honored.

Being a Nafia thug was a pretty good gig for Paddy. For the first time he was responsible for others. He employed one malefactor and three miscreants.

Oh, they were carefree days for Paddy. Some of the best days of his life.

Each morning he would get up in the afternoon, enjoy a bowl of oatmeal and several shots of whiskey, and then make the rounds of small shops and kiosks, extorting "protection" money.

Paddy had a certain charm that even his victims appreciated. One of them, Luigi MacMackenzie, testified in court that Paddy had never once threatened to kill him if he didn't pay up. Instead, he always phrased his threats politely.

"Which would you prefer, Mr. MacMackenzie? That I beat you with a brick until you can't talk without drooling? Or would you prefer to pay up?"

It was these small courtesies that his victims always appreciated.

Unfortunately Paddy was not as good at managing his subordinates. In fact, the reluctant conclusion of the Nafia bosses was that Paddy would never be a people person.

So his career took an unexpected turn. Rather than being promoted along the path from thug to marauder to pillager—a path that might eventually have led to a comfortable life as a crime boss—Paddy was guided onto a lonelier path.

This path led from thug to backstabber to assassin. No one really liked assassins. One of their chief jobs was to take out fellow Nafia members who were too soft, or squealed to the cops, or asked too many questions, or looked funny.

Paddy acted like he didn't care. "Hey, I never wanted a nice suburban home in New Jersey with a blond wife and two difficult kids. I don't even like onion rings."

No one knew what that last remark meant, but who was going to question him? Paddy had become a dangerous guy.

It was about this time that an event occurred that altered the course of Paddy's life: the local boss of the Black Hand invited him to join him at his country club for a round of golf.

This gentleman was known as Six Toes Ricotta.

Their golf game changed Paddy's life forever.

Eleven

Down into the dark they stumbled, tripping on steep steps. Stefan sagged in Mack's and Jarrah's arms and barely motored his feet forward.

Mack glanced back and saw the nine-dragon wall sliding back up with barely a sound. An astonished guard gaped down at him, shook his head like it was all a dream, and chopped at an elf.

Then, total darkness.

The air smelled of mold and dust and rotten eggs.

Mack shifted his grip on Stefan. He held up his phone, trying to see with the dim light. It didn't really work; the space was too big. Which was bad, because right then Mack started thinking about his very least favorite story: "The Cask of Amontillado," in which a guy gets walled up in a basement.

Mack whimpered.

Then, a voice!

"Is that the new iPhone, or the earlier model?"

A girl's voice. And she seemed to actually expect an answer.

"I . . . I'm not sure," Mack admitted.

A match flared. Mack had an impression of a heart-shaped face and almond eyes and black hair.

The match burned. It lit a torch. The torch was then carried to the wall, where another torch lit and then, like dominoes falling, the flame went flying from torch to torch off into the distance.

"Xiao Long," the girl said. "You may call me Xiao."

She was dressed in a tight-fitting, full-length, gold-embroidered turquoise silk dress.

"I'm Mack," Mack said. "This is Jarrah. And Stefan. Who needs a doctor."

"I can see that."

"How can we get out of here and find a hospital?"

Xiao looked at him for what felt like a very long time. Then she said, "Ah." As though she just got something. As though she didn't like what she had just realized.

"Come with me," Xiao said. "I will take you to my parents."

"Is one of them a doctor?"

Xiao had already turned away to lead them. She hesitated. "They are both . . . well, they will be helpful. Or fatal."

Mack was pretty sure he hadn't heard that last word quite right. Because obviously, why would she be saying her parents could be fatal?

They walked down a long hallway. It was quite wide, as wide as the nine-dragon wall had been. It headed downhill at a steep angle. At the end of the hallway were three enormous elevators. They didn't have doors; they were just platforms suspended on cables as thick as Stefan's bicep.

There were no buttons to push. Once they were all aboard the platform, it dropped. Slowly at first. Then faster, faster, so fast that the shaft walls were a blur of stone and rock.

The elevator slowed, stopped, and Xiao led the way off the platform. Now they faced a set of massive steel doors decorated with what had to be real gold filigree. You could drive a moving van through those doors. And you could make a million wedding rings out of the swirling gold framing.

As Xiao approached, the doors swung silently inward onto bright light and lush color and a smell of flowers.

Mack, Stefan, and Jarrah reached the threshold and froze. They were standing at the top of a long descending ramp that extended for what had to be two football fields in length.

It led down to a cavern so vast that at first Mack could not believe it was underground. It was impossibly big. Big like the Grand Canyon. Big. Really big. In fact, you could have sawed a giant line around the Forbidden City and dropped the whole thing crashing down into this cavern and have room left over for a couple of major malls.

Mack, his jaw open, counted nine massive palaces,

each done up in red and azure and gold and green. Each palace had acres and acres of grass lawn and cute, well-trimmed trees. A river meandered through it all, like a sparkling liquid road. Light-colored bricks bordered the river and occasionally spread out to form tree-shaded plazas.

There were no other roads or pathways. No cars. No bikes. No people, as far as Mack could tell.

The sky—the roof of this ridiculously large cave—was painted blue, and decorated with what had to be millions of paintings of people and animals and mountains and dragons. Like the Sistine Chapel but so big the entire Sistine Chapel ceiling would have been one drawing.

From the very center of the blue ceiling hung a steel pot so huge that blue whales could have floated around inside. But the pot-in-the-sky did not contain water; it contained light. It shone through artful cutouts and reflected onto the ceiling. An artificial sun.

"Welcome to Long Xiang," Xiao said.

Stefan opened his eyes and struggled to focus. "Huh," he said, and slumped again.

"Crikey," Jarrah said.

"Whoa," Mack said.

Xiao stood aside so they could see better. Just then something that looked an awful lot like a very big snake began to emerge from one of the nine palaces. It was hard to judge size from this distance, but it looked about as big around as a redwood tree and as long as four or five city buses end to end.

It was brilliant yellow with scales that flashed in the light of the artificial sun.

It was not a snake. For one thing, it was far too big to be a snake. Plus it had four stubby lizard legs. Each leg ended in five claws.

Its head was almost horselike. But it had two horns that twisted back from its brow, horns that must have been as long as flagpoles. It had a mouth at once fierce and laughing, as if the creature found many things amusing, and then ate those amusing things.

It slithered and squirmed from the palace.

Then, without wings or jet engines or rockets, it slithered right up into the sky.

"That's like . . . that's like a . . . ," Jarrah said. But she was baffled as to just what the creature might be.

"A giant flying snake?" Mack offered.

"Not a snake!" Xiao said a little angrily, like the idea was disgusting. "That is my father."

"Your father?" Jarrah said with a disbelieving laugh.

"But he's a—whatever," Mack said. "And you're . . ." Mack felt a warning prickling on the back of his neck. Mack was good at noticing things. He'd been distracted by the unreal sights before him. But still he'd heard a slight shushing, slithering sound coming from Xiao's direction. And he'd noticed that her name, Xiao Long, had the same word—*Long*—as the name of this place, Long Xiang.

Slowly Mack turned.

Xiao was much smaller than her father. But even more brightly colored, mostly a delicate turquoise with gold streaks. And scales. And the four stubby legs.

"Jarrah," Mack said.

"Ya ah ah!" Jarrah cried.

"*Long*," Mack said. "What does that mean in Mandarin?"

"*Dragon*," Xiao said. "I am Xiao Long—Young Dragon. And this, Mack and Jarrah and Stefan, is the place no human has seen in centuries. Long Xiang: Dragon Home."

Stefan, his voice a whisper, said, "Dude, I think I'm dying."

He fell from Mack's grip and began to roll down the long ramp.

Twelve

The vast yellow dragon snaked through the sky.

The much smaller turquoise dragon—Xiao—suddenly took flight and soared up toward him.

And Stefan rolled down the ramp. With each revolution he left a small red stain on the stone.

Mack and Jarrah pelted after him, but he had picked up a fair amount of speed and the ramp was steep. It was like trying to catch a ball rolling downhill away from you.

But then, down came both dragons, Xiao and her father. They landed on the ramp in front of Stefan.

Mack felt the earth bounce from the impact of the landing.

Stefan rolled right into the giant dragon's giant claw. He came to a stop.

Mack and Jarrah arrived breathless in the shadow of the monstrous scaled beast. Its head was as big as an SUV. Its eyes were like beach balls.

Angry beach balls.

"I have asked my father to help this boy," Xiao said. "He has agreed."

"However . . . ," the giant yellow dragon said.

It was a single word, but it was a big word. The sound blast blew Jarrah's hair back. It made Mack take a step back. It vibrated through his body from the ground up and from the air down and sort of reverberated back and forth so that he was like a Jell-O cube in an earthquake.

"However," Xiao said, "this does not mean you might not be killed later."

"If you can help him, do it!" Jarrah said. "We'll take our chances."

Xiao's father nodded his huge head. Then, with a

delicateness and care Mack would not have believed possible, he raised one leg and extended one claw and with perfect precision sliced Stefan's shirt open.

Mack winced when he saw the wound. Jarrah let loose a small cry of dismay. It was worse when you could see it clearly. Mostly because you could see that the hole was very close to Stefan's heart.

How was he going to live with himself if he'd gotten Stefan killed? That fear wasn't a phobia; it was something different. Darker, more stomach churning and less panic inducing.

Xiao's father then stuck the tip of his claw right into the hole.

"You'll kill him!" Jarrah cried.

The huge dragon's beach ball eyes, with vertical slits that reminded Mack of a cat's eye—and into which a full-grown cat could fit quite easily—flicked toward Jarrah.

"Silence, girl," the dragon said, and again, spoken in that very large voice, it had the effect of making both Jarrah and Mack think they'd better just stand there quietly until called upon.

The dragon's claw plunged deep into the wound.

Blood bubbled around it.

Then the claw was slowly, slowly withdrawn. It came away without a sign of blood. And when it was fully withdrawn, Stefan's chest was dry and normal except for a small pink scar.

The scar was in the shape of a Chinese character.

Xiao laughed, and the giant dragon made what was possibly a smile, or a grimace of rage—it was hard to tell.

"The character means 'lucky,'" Xiao explained.

Stefan's eyes opened. He stared straight up at the biggest living thing he would ever see. Which was why, in shock and amazement, and obviously overcome with emotion, he said, "Huh."

Then he hopped up, looked down at the scar, and said, "Cool. It's like, better than a tatt."

Jarrah rushed over and gave him a quick hug. A hug that embarrassed both her and Stefan. And Mack.

"So, what's this about killing us?" Mack asked Xiao. "That was a joke, right?"

It was hard to read her expression. Dragons are inscrutable, to put it mildly. "We'll talk," she said cryptically. "First, to my home. I'll take you, Mack.

My father will carry Jarrah and Stefan."

Daddy dragon closed a giant hand—or whatever it was—around Jarrah and another around Stefan, and without any sign of effort simply rose and slithered away into the sky.

It was a bit more awkward for Xiao. Her claws were nowhere near as big.

"Climb onto my back," she instructed Mack.

Mack said, "Um . . . uh . . . ," and other very intelligent things. He'd never even gone to a school-sponsored dance with a female. But in the end he did what he was told and managed to straddle Xiao's back.

She didn't feel slimy. Not that he had any strong opinions on what dragons should feel like. But he was still surprised that the scales were dry. They felt a little like thick leaves. Like maybe they were living tissue but they could be plastic, too.

Beneath the scales was all sinewy muscle.

"Hold on to my horns," Xiao said.

Her horns were smaller than her father's, and twisted like swirly soft-serve ice-cream cones.

Mack held on to Xiao's horns. He squeezed his knees tight. He thought about closing his eyes and then realized, no, that would be stupid: better to know if she was crashing into something.

And then, without straining or even grunting, Xiao simply slithered up off the ramp. Up they went in a sinuous move that reminded Mack of when he'd seen sidewinders out in the Arizona desert.

In seconds they were halfway to the blue-painted ceiling, on a path to pass just beneath the light-filled cauldron.

Thirteen

The palace—it seemed to be the largest of the nine—was quite a place.

It looked a bit like some of the palaces in the Forbidden City, but as if they were the original size and the Forbidden City palaces were miniature versions.

It was big. Mack had been to see the Diamondbacks play at Chase Field in Phoenix. This palace was like that.

Unlike Chase Field, the palace was red. Red on the outside, red and gold on the inside. Not gold paint, Mack suspected, but actual gold. Chairs of gold, lamps of gold, decorative trim of gold.

They were deposited in a room so cavernous you could park an aircraft carrier on that polished floor. At the far end was a throne on a platform.

Xiao's father slithered and walked to that throne and climbed up onto it. He sort of sat and sort of just draped across it, curling his tail in a coil below.

"That has got to be the biggest chair in the world," Jarrah said.

"If it was me, I'd have an awesome flat-screen to go with that easy chair," Stefan said.

"My father doesn't watch a lot of TV," Xiao said. She was once again a slim, pretty girl with thoughtful eyes and long black hair. "Follow me."

They took a walk—about a five-minute walk—to get close to the throne. Mack was not exactly convinced he wanted to get too close. The huge yellow dragon had saved Stefan's life. But who knew when he might get hostile?

Or hungry.

As they got closer, something that Mack had thought might be a small palace all on its own began to seem more like a very large desk. Very large pens—not ballpoints, not felt-tips, more like brushes really—stood in ornate holders.

Occupying a huge—okay, look, let's just assume everything here was huge—wall shelf were books and rolled-up scrolls.

"My father's books and poems," Xiao said with a wave of her hand.

"Has Harry Potter been translated into Dragon?" Mack asked.

"My father reads all languages," Xiao said a little snippily. "But he only writes in Chinese characters. Those are all books that he has written. Poems, plays, stories, history books, observations of nature. His specialty is songbirds. He knows everything about songbirds."

As if on cue, two bright yellow birds went fluttering past, circled, and landed on one of the dragon's hands. The birds, at least, were normal size.

Finally Xiao came to a stop. They were still maybe fifty feet from the closest coil of the great dragon's tail.

His giant head was far above.

Xiao said, "Father, I would like to make a proper introduction. May I present Mack, Stefan, and Jarrah."

Then she turned politely to Mack and said, "This is my honored father, Huang Long, King of Dragons."

Mack stared. It was hard not to. He was being stared at, so he pretty much had to either stare back or curl up in a fetal position on the floor and whimper like a baby.

"What do I call him?" Mack whispered.

"You don't," Xiao whispered back. "He talks. You answer."

"Right."

Huang Long, the Dragon King, spoke. This time his voice was a bit quieter—he was using his inside voice—so it was only as loud as a rock band, not as loud as standing next to a jet engine.

"Two of you possess the *enlightened puissance*," Huang Long said. "Do not be alarmed that I see this: I see most things."

It wasn't a question, so Mack and his friends kept quiet. He wanted to make a joke about how, with eyes that big, the dragon probably did see things pretty well. But Mack suspected this wasn't the time for teasing.

"You are of the Magnifica," Huang Long said.

He sighed. It was a deep sigh that seemed to first suck a blimpload of air in, and then let a blimpload of air out in what would be a strong gale or a moderate hurricane.

"So," the Dragon King said slowly, "it is time. The Pale Queen rises again. And who will stop her now? Long has she waited and plotted and prepared. Her allies are many. Her powers great. Her evil without limit. And her foul daughter has come fully into her own."

Still no question. But Mack was amazed to hear all this. Because it was kind of convincing when you heard it from a spectral bathroom apparition. But it was really, really convincing when you heard it from the King of Dragons.

"You have come to find the third of your number," Huang Long said. "And alas, you have found the one."

"You're one of the Magnificent Twelve?" It was Jarrah, sounding both amazed and hopeful. "I mean, with you along, I like our chances a lot better."

The Dragon King blinked. Blinked again.

Mack held his breath. But Huang Long decided not to take offense at being interrupted.

"No, little fool, not me," he said. And then, he laughed.

You know what an earthquake feels like? (Probably not.) That's what the dragon's laugh was like. The ground shook, the walls vibrated, Mack's insides were shaken and stirred.

Huang Long wiped tears of laughter away with the tip of his tail. "I am five thousand years old," he explained. "It's not the Magnificent Five Thousand, it's the Magnificent Twelve. And I am not a warrior or a hero. I am a scholar. In my own humble way."

Now he focused only on his daughter, looking at her with giant, suddenly sad eyes. "We have sensed that this day might come, Daughter. Twelve short but joyful years have passed since your mother and I had the joy of seeing you break from the egg."

Xiao bowed her head. "I am ready, Father."

The Dragon King shook his head slowly. "No, Daughter, you are not. No one is ready to face the

Mother of All Monsters. When I was young, she was already old. But if ever one could be ready, you are."

Mack saw tears in Xiao's eyes. "Thank you, Father," she whispered.

Mack's phone rang. "Really?" he asked Xiao. "You have cell phone service down here?" He glanced at the display. The golem calling again.

It wasn't a good time. He muted the phone. It continued to vibrate softly in his pocket.

"You may be as ready as can be, but I am not ready to see you go. And your mother will be angry with me for letting you. But we have duties, duties you understand well despite your age."

"We are the defenders of learning and culture, of respect for our elders and for tradition," Xiao said, like she was reciting from memory.

Huang Long nodded his head. His pride in his daughter was clear despite the fact that he was, after all, a dragon. But he was troubled, too.

"What do you know of your destiny?" Huang Long asked Mack.

"Not much," Mack admitted. "All I know is there's this Pale Queen, and she was locked up, like, three

MACK WAS MISTAKEN. THERE WAS NO ENGLISH PAPER IN HIS COMPUTER. NO PAPER OF ANY KIND. I DON'T THINK THERE WAS EVEN ANY ROOM IN THERE FOR A PAPER. I TRIED TO CALL MACK. NO ANSWER.

thousand years ago. And now she's getting out. And we're supposed to stop her."

Huang Long looked troubled, hesitant, like he wasn't quite sure how much he should say. Then he took a deep breath and sighed a long, long sigh. A long sigh.

Dragons have very big lungs.

"You must learn the Vargran tongue. Those who have the *enlightened puissance* can use those words to magical effect. But only when they are young. Too young, and the *enlightened puissance* is too undisciplined. Too old, and the mind becomes too rigid. There is a very narrow window of opportunity."

"Yes, we've used some Vargran words," Mack said.

"Oh, yeah," Stefan agreed. Then he made a whooshing noise, mimicked a fireball exploding, and pointed at Mack. "*Boom.* It was epic."

"Grimluk has sent you here to find my daughter," Huang Long said. "But perhaps even more importantly so that you may study Vargran. We have a very ancient Vargran text." He frowned at the shelves of books. "That's the one. The old book bound in red-dyed alligator skin."

Mack followed the dragon's gaze and saw the book. The book that would teach them all the secrets of Vargran. The book that might give them the power to save the entire human race.

The book that was roughly five feet wide, seven feet long, and two feet thick.

"Do you have it on a flash drive?" Mack asked. "Or maybe as a download?"

Xiao shook her head at him. "It's not the kind of thing you get at the iBooks store."

"You must stay with us awhile and study," Huang Long said. "In a few short months—"

"Sir, we have thirty-five days. Maybe thirty-four, depending on how late it is."

"Ah." The huge dragon was taken aback. He began counting on his talons. "Yes, thirty-four days. Math was always my weakest area of study."

"Father, we have to go soon or risk failure," Xiao said.

The dragon looked pained. "Your mother and I hoped this day would never come, though we felt it might. I still had hopes that you would grow to wise old age, here in our home. That I would one day read with joy your own poems and books, and learn from your studies. That day may yet come, but you will be forever changed by the struggle ahead."

Xiao said nothing, too overcome to trust herself to speak.

Huang Long then bent far forward. Mack thought he was going to give her a kiss—not that dragons have lips exactly—but he leaned down toward Stefan.

"You," Huang Long said. "I feel your courage. Will you protect my daughter?"

Stefan did not seem the least bit frightened. It took more than a giant dragon to scare Stefan. But he seemed solemn.

"Dude," Stefan said to the King of Dragons, "you saved my life. I totally owe you. I'll get her back to you in one piece. Or die trying."

That seemed to satisfy Huang Long. He sat back on his throne. "Go, my most perfect songbird, say farewell to your mother. Then, with these, your companions, assemble the Magnificent Twelve and save the world."

It was a beautiful moment. Mack wished he had the nerve to take a picture.

But the moment didn't last long.

There came a thump. Like a bomb going off, but not right in the room.

And suddenly there was another dragon rushing into the room. Not quite as big as Huang Long, but definitely greener and somehow more feminine.

"Mother!" Xiao cried.

Mother dragon yelled something in a language Mack did not understand. Huang Long's head snapped up. His eyes blazed.

Xiao spun to Mack and said, "Invaders! They've blown up the nine-dragon wall!"

Fourteen

STILL A LONG TIME AGO . . .

Six Toes Ricotta was the *capo di tutti capi*, the head Black Hand boss for New York. He was accompanied by two of his boys, Bad Breath Caprino and Fatface Pecarino.

Despite his usual caution, Paddy was excited by the invitation. It could only be a job offer. Lately the Black Hand had been growing quickly—more quickly than the Nafia—and Paddy thought he might have a better career with them.

Plus, the Black Hand had recently begun allowing its members to date. Which meant that Black Hand members could go see movies without looking lonely and pathetic. They could go out to restaurants without the waiters looking at them with pity.

The Black Hand believed you could be a ruthless killer and still find love. But the Nafia was sticking to its traditional position, which was opposed to any chance at personal happiness.

It was a beautiful day. The sun was high in the sky as the four of them drove in a steam-powered car to the golf course.

Paddy had never been on a golf course before. It was green and lush and clean. It reminded him a little of County Grind. But with fewer hovels and no pigs.

Fatface had brought a cooler. Of course, this being a long time ago, it was a steam-powered cooler.

"Have a drink, Paddy," Six Toes said. "Fatface! Give the kid a drink."

And standing there on that endless green grass with a glass of chilled wine in his hand, Paddy felt mighty good.

"You play much golf?" Six Toes asked politely.

"No. But back in the Old Country we had a game we played called gopher-and-hole." Paddy took a refreshing swig and almost smiled at the memory. "We'd cut the head off a gopher, carry it a hundred paces away, and try to knock the head back into the gopher's hole using clubs made out of starched pig intestines."

The three Black Hand criminals stared at him.

"Sure an' it were a grand sport, so it was, so it was," Paddy reminisced.

But the three hoods erupted into derisive laughter. "Starched pig intestines? Ah-ha-ha-ha!"

"You're really a rube, aren't you?" Bad Breath Caprino said.

"What a bumpkin!"

"Heh," Six Toes snarked, "what can you expect from an oat eater?"

Paddy's smile disappeared. A small fire was burning inside him. He blushed. Which he had never done before.

"Let's get started," Six Toes said. And then he spoke the words that would change his own life and Paddy's, too. He said, "Grab me my driver from my golf bag. Oh, wait! You wouldn't recognize a driver, would you?

It's not the same as a pig intestine. Ha-ha-ha. You wouldn't know a driver from a . . . from a nine iron."

Paddy swallowed his boiling rage.

He went to the steam-powered golf cart, found the golf bag, rummaged through for a few seconds, found what he was looking for, and stalked back to the three laughing Black Handers.

"This," Paddy said, "is a driver."

He swung the driver so hard that Fatface wasn't fat anymore.

"No! No!" Six Toes cried.

Paddy tossed the driver aside.

"And this," Paddy said, "is a nine iron."

It's best not to dwell on what Paddy did with the nine iron. Suffice it to say that five minutes later there was a sudden opening in the leadership of the Black Hand.

It was such a bad afternoon for the Black Hand that—under new leadership—they reorganized and renamed their organization. Out of respect for Nafia assassin Paddy Trout, they called their new criminal gang the Mafia.

And Paddy had earned the nickname that would follow him for the rest of his long life: Nine Iron.

Fifteen

Huang Long, the Dragon King, could move pretty fast for a creature the size of a subway train. With a whoosh he flew overhead. Mother dragon flew with him.

Xiao grabbed Mack's arm and pulled him along, even as she swiftly changed from human back to dragon. In seconds Mack was airborne on Xiao's scaly back, zooming crazily through the palace in the wake of the first family of Dragon Land.

They burst through the door and out into the open.

Instantly Mack spotted a small army of creatures—Tong Elves, Skirrit, and Lepercons—rushing down the long ramp. Smoke billowed behind them.

A dragon the color of ripe plums swirled before them, and even from this distance Mack could hear a stunningly loud dragon voice shouting, "Back! This is Dragon Home!"

Two of the Skirrit were hauling an odd, ornate tube, like a cannon lifted off its wheels, or like a really heavy bazooka.

They stopped, rested the barrel on the backs of two Tong Elves, and took aim at the purple dragon.

Mack saw the explosion before he heard the bang. A spray of tiny bright pellets—they sparkled like diamonds—hit the purple dragon.

"Sizzle cannon!" Xiao yelled.

Instantly the dragon fell to the ground.

Xiao cried out in terror and rage. Mack could feel her muscles tense beneath her scales.

Huang Long looked back at his daughter. "Go! I will take care of this!"

"Father, no!" Xiao cried. "I can fight!"

"It's not us they want," Huang Long snapped. "It's

the humans! Get them to safety. Take the barge! And remember: the key is the Vargran tongue. Each of the Twelve will have a different resonance of the *enlightened puissance*, a different special ability. But it will all rest on Vargran!"

"Go, little one!" her mother cried. "You must fulfill your destiny! But keep up with your algebra homework!"

Xiao started to argue; Mack could almost feel the defiance. But with a shudder Xiao said, "Yes, Father. Yes, Mother."

She turned suddenly, practically leaving Mack's stomach behind. They sped back to where a very frustrated Stefan and Jarrah waited.

Xiao landed and changed to her human look. Which, by the way, had some creepy moments. Half dragon, half girl is not a good look for anyone. "We should run," she panted. "I can't carry the three of you."

Mack didn't need to be asked twice. The four of them ran. Across manicured lawns, across decorative arched bridges, shortcutting through a palace done up in pale pink and gold lace.

Overhead the dragons flew with a whoosh of wind

to confront the menace.

"Can't your dad just hose them down with his fire breath?" Jarrah asked as they ran.

Mack could see her point. He'd spotted at least half a dozen dragons so far. It was hard to see how anything could stand up to them.

"Fire breath?" Xiao snorted. "What, like Eragon? Like in Tolkien? Does my father look like Smaug to you?" Then in a somewhat less offended tone, "The fire breathing? That's our western cousins, not us. We are not those dragons. We are not barbarians. First, my father will attempt to reason with the invaders."

They were nearing one of the towering walls of the cave. Mack spotted an opening, like the mouth of a cave, bordered in carved wood. It was simple, nothing ornate.

They were racing alongside the gentle river that wandered through Dragon Home, and Mack realized that the river must flow out through that opening. He couldn't see it very clearly from this angle. He couldn't see much of anything because sweat was stinging his eyes.

But he did notice the four Skirrit bounding along

the far side of the river, keeping pace on their crazy grasshopper legs, taking twenty-yard steps, racing to cut them off.

And he noticed that at least two of them had something that looked a little like guns—but could also have been bent soda cans.

Skreeet!

That made everyone miss a step. No one had ever heard that sound before. And the missed step saved them.

A spray of crystalline pellets went shooting by, just in front of them.

"Owww!" Jarrah cried.

She stared at the back of her hand (still running, of course; she was curious about the pain, but not curious enough to stand around examining herself).

Skirrit

www.themag12.com

"It's a . . . a thing!" Jarrah cried.

"Get it off you!" Xiao yelled.

Jarrah picked at it with her finger.

"No, no! Not with your finger! It'll sizzle your finger, too!"

As she ran, Jarrah dug out a coin from her pocket and used the edge of it to pry the tiny, painful bead from her hand.

"Are they shooting at us with cans of Mountain Dew?" Stefan asked.

"Sizzle guns," Xiao said grimly. "The pellets are like tiny magnets. They try to come together, and they put out a bubbly acid to eat anything that gets in the way. Imagine a hundred of them hitting you!"

Imagining this helped Mack and the others run faster. But not as fast as the Skirrit, who were now ahead of them on the far bank and would easily cut them off where the river entered the wall.

"Can you all swim?" Xiao cried. Then added, "Underwater?"

No one answered.

The Skirrit were standing still now, blocking the way, aiming their sizzle guns.

Xiao leaped and broke the river surface with a perfect knifelike dive. Jarrah was right behind her, equally athletic.

Stefan and Mack hit the water together—more cannonball than Olympic racing dive.

Mack swallowed a little water, fought down the desperate urge to cough, opened his eyes, and saw three sets of shoes kicking away from him.

He leveled off, tried not to think about drowning, and swam hard after them through lovely aquamarine water.

Turning slightly, Mack saw refracted Skirrit faces peering down into the water.

He kept kicking.

Ahead was darkness like a wall. He saw Stefan's shoes kicking. He followed.

Through the water he heard churning and someone shouting and, from farther away now, the furious cries of the Skirrit.

He swam until his lungs burned and his muscles grew weak from lack of oxygen and his brain swirled. Then, when he had no other choice, he surfaced and sucked air like it was the last breath he would ever take.

Stefan's strong hands grabbed his wet shirt and his belt and hauled him onto a dry surface. He coughed up river water, exhausted. But at least there were no Skirrit.

What there was, was a very odd boat.

Xiao was speaking respectfully to the "boat." And of course the boat was answering her with equally grave politeness.

Mack hung his head down between his knees.

"Just like, five minutes of normal. Just five minutes. That would be great."

Stefan laughed happily. "Dude, we have moved out of normal. We live in cuh-razeee now!"

Sixteen

The boat—the barge, as Huang Long had called it; the royal barge, in fact—was not quite what Mack had expected. For one thing, it was alive.

Above the water it looked kind of like a boat. It had sides that might be wood or woodlike. It had a deck that was hard and firm underfoot. It had a tall mast, and that's where things began to look weird. The mast was very obviously not a tree trunk but a spur of white bone, slightly bowed and tapering.

Below the waterline Mack could glimpse the rest of the barge. It looked a bit like a whale, very large, tinged blue. Toward the stern was not one set of flukes but three vertical tails, like a shark's tail. Times three.

And at the front was a long, sinewy neck ending in a head and face like a very large pug dog.

"We'll need seats, Barge," Xiao said to the pug face.

"Ah! Then we'll be moving at speed?"

"Yes. Full speed."

The pug face grinned. "Ah, yes!"

The deck, which had seemed almost like wood, was revealed as living flesh as it rippled and formed rudimentary benches.

"Sit. Hold on tight," Xiao commanded.

Mack took the seat beside Xiao.

"Ready," Xiao said, and before the last syllable had stopped reverberating through the air, the barge launched. Like a roller coaster out of a power chute.

A huge bow wave went up, forming walls of spray to their right and left. The sail filled with wind, despite the fact that there was no wind, and the barge swooshed away like a rocket.

Mack was slammed against his seat. Xiao grinned

at him. "The barge never gets to go full speed. He lives for this."

They rocketed down the tunnel, water drenching the rock sides and roof. After a while an area opened up on the right, a sort of diorama. It blew by in a flash, and they were back in the gloomy tunnel.

"What was that?"

Xiao shrugged. "Like a museum: great moments in history. Normally we'd be going slower and we could enjoy the displays. They keep the trip from getting too boring."

"Where are we going?" Jarrah asked. She looked as happy as the pug head, whose tongue was hanging out about three feet, like a dog on a car ride.

"To the wall," Xiao said. "There we can get a flight to our next stop."

"What's our next stop?" Jarrah asked.

Xiao looked puzzled. "Don't you know?"

"We don't exactly have a map," Mack said.

"What do you have?"

"Some old dude who talks to us from bathroom fixtures," Mack said.

Xiao stared at him. Blinked. Blinked again.

"Yeah," Mack said, "that's what we think of it, too." He shrugged. "Look, I'm sure Grimluk would lay it all out for us if he could. But the dude's three thousand years old, and I think he's doing the best he can. And the bad guys kind of keep the pressure on us, you know? When we were back at school just finding out about this, or at Uluru, or when we were talking to your dad . . . I mean, it's not like we ever get a lot of downtime to sit around and plan things out. We have thirty-four days, and the Pale Queen is trying hard to make sure we don't even have one day."

"I didn't intend any criticism," Xiao said mildly.

Mack sighed. He felt discouraged. This whole thing had been impossible from the start. It was getting more impossible with each passing day. With each hour.

"Anyway," Mack said, "all I know right now is 'egg rocks.' And hopefully that leads us to number four. And we kind of have to figure they'll come after us there, too."

"Hey," Jarrah said. "No worries: we're not dead yet."

"And we're having fun!" Stefan said. Then, when

he saw the extremely dubious faces turned toward him, he added in a less enthusiastic voice, "Well, I am."

"Have you Googled the 'egg rocks' thing?" Xiao asked.

"We think it's in Germany. A place called Externsteine."

They blew along at what had to be ever-increasing speed, because now the water flying from the bow had been turned to steam. Friction heat.

"This is excellent," Stefan said. "You guys ever water-ski off this thing?"

Xiao did not seem amused. "Is he one of us?" she asked Mack.

"Not exactly," Mack said. The question made him uncomfortable. "He's . . . Well, he used to be my bully."

"Your bully?"

"Yeah, he was the toughest kid in the school. We got to know each other because he was always beating me up."

"Is that how American kids get to know each other?"

"I wouldn't say it's the most common way. Sometimes we just walk up to someone and, you know, say hi or whatever."

"I see," Xiao said, although Mack doubted she did.

"So. You're a dragon."

"Yes."

"But you're also a girl."

"No, I'm a dragon. But I can make myself into a girl. It's how I go to school."

"You go to school? Dragon school?"

"No. Human school. In the outside world." She pointed upward. "Up there. Although not directly up there, because we are far beyond the city now."

"Why do you go to human school? To learn human stuff?"

"Not really," Xiao said. "It's to learn basic things. And wrong things."

"That's why I go to school, too: to learn wrong things," Mack said. Xiao didn't seem to get that he was joking. He was beginning to fear that she had no sense of humor. Normally Mack would find this very off-putting. It made it almost hard for him to relate, to talk to a person. But he didn't feel that way about Xiao, possibly because she was a dragon.

"So you're one of us," he said. "I mean, one of the

Magnificent Twelve."

"Yes. I've known it for some time now. We dragons may know some things you humans don't. Like, well, like just about everything except technology."

"We know other stuff, too," Mack said.

Xiao looked skeptically at him. "Tell me the truth: before all this started, you only believed in the things you could see and touch and feel. Right? You knew nothing about the wonders and the terrors that lie hidden in the unseen places of the Earth."

"Well, I didn't know there were dragons living under the Forbidden City, that's true. Or dragons any-where. Or Lepercons. Or Tong Elves. Or Skirrit. Or some princess named Risky."

"A princess named Risky?" Xiao said, puzzled.

Mack was pleased to discover something he knew that Xiao did not. "I think her full name is Ereskigal."

Xiao's eyes froze into a stare. She didn't move, except for a cheek muscle. It twitched.

"Ereskigal?" She held her breath, then let it out in a gasp. "You encountered Ereskigal?"

"Yeah. We weren't exactly friends. And I kind of had to destroy her." He had conflicted feelings about that. On the one hand, it seemed kind of creepy to brag about killing anyone or anything. On the other hand, he'd managed to take down a very, very scary person.

Xiao laughed. "You did not kill her. At least not the way you think."

"Hey," Stefan interjected from the seat in front of them. "Mack fried her butt. Zap! Shock and awe! Smoke and ash! Pow! So awesome."

"You don't know much, do you?" Xiao said.

To Mack's amazement, Stefan's face sort of crumpled. If Mack hadn't known better, he'd have thought Stefan was a little intimidated by Xiao. "No," he mumbled. "I don't."

"Ereskigal, or as some say it, Ereshkigal, is Morgan le Fay, Kali, Persephone, and Hel."

"She's Hel all right," Jarrah muttered.

"She is not dead. Ereskigal must be killed twelve times, each time in a different way. Unless you killed her twelve times, she is not gone."

Mack glanced nervously over his shoulder. Even Risky couldn't possibly keep up with the barge.

Although now that he noticed it, the barge was

starting to slow down.

"We're almost there," Xiao said. "We'll pass as tourists at the wall. It's morning now. We have to walk for a way along the wall; the dragon we're to meet doesn't like the river, so he lives a short distance away."

The barge was definitely going slower.

Then it stopped beside a dock. Xiao led the way off the barge. She paused to thank the creature. Then began a long climb up a spiral staircase. At the top of about a thousand steps (actual number 812), a tube hung from the arched stone ceiling. It was brass and green and ended in eyepieces. Xiao took a look through the eyepieces.

"It's clear," she said.

Now they climbed a bronze ladder. Xiao pushed up against what looked like a blank stone ceiling. It lifted with surprising ease.

They climbed out onto a wall. But not just any wall. The Great Wall of China.

This was a wall that, back in the days when it was all still standing, ran more than five thousand miles. About ten feet thick, maybe thirty feet tall except for the frequent towers.

Steep, green, triangular mountains tumbled together. They weren't that tall, but there were a lot of them. Like a bunch of fuzzy green blocks all jumbled together.

The wall snaked right across these mountains, up one side, down the next, up again, down again, and whee, around to catch the next mountain.

It reminded Mack a little of the dragons. Sinewy and snakelike and strong, with stones and cobbles making the scales.

"Big wall," Stefan commented.

"Yes," Xiao agreed. "An enormous structure built by humans. A sacred place of great power. Millions labored for many years to build it. And many of those who built it died in the process. Their bones are now beneath our feet."

Stefan carefully stepped aside.

"I meant all through the wall, not just right here beneath your feet," Xiao explained. "When workers died, they were added to the wall."

She looked at Stefan as if expecting a response, but he had turned away and was no longer listening.

"This way," Xiao said, and pointed downhill.

"Yeah, let's go that way," Stefan said. "Because you

know what? I think dragon girl is right. Risky? She's not all that dead."

Slowly Mack turned. The hair on the back of his head was standing up.

There, at the top of the closest mountain behind them, stood Princess Ereskigal.

She waved.

Waved like she and Mack were old friends.

"Hi, Mack!" she cried cheerfully. "Stay right there. I'm coming to kill you!"

Seventeen

DID WE MENTION IT WAS A LONG TIME AGO. . . .

In order to be named an official, full-fledged Nafia assassin, Paddy "Nine Iron" Trout had to do some traveling. His bosses gave him a choice.

"Bottomless pit in Greece or volcano in Italy?"

"Say what?"

"You gotta meet the boss: she makes the final decisions on major promotions like this."

"What if she doesn't like me?" Nine Iron asked.

"Well, then she'll have you for lunch."

Nine Iron didn't think this sounded too bad. Until he considered that *Have you for lunch* could be taken two different ways.

"Volcano," Nine Iron said.

So he was booked for a trip on the zeppelin *Furzlassen*. Zeppelins were giant airships. Basically you had a steel frame, and a giant skin stretched tight over that steel frame, and then the whole thing was filled with sacks of a lighter-than-air gas like helium, which was perfectly safe, or hydrogen, which could blow up if you so much as looked at it sideways.

Naturally the *Furzlassen* was filled with hydrogen.

The whole thing altogether was shaped like a cigar, one hundred feet in diameter and about eight hundred feet long. The bottom of the zeppelin had passenger and crew compartments like sleeper cars on a train. There was also a bar, a restaurant, and a smoking room. Which, given that the ship was being floated by giant sacks containing 3.7 million cubic feet of highly flammable gas, may not have been a great idea.

It was a fine trip. Nine Iron was booked into a

windowless second-class room. Unimaginable luxury for a man who, as a child, had traveled seventh class.

But Nine Iron had gotten so he enjoyed a degree of luxury, so he moved up to a first-class cabin that became available right after the original passenger was tossed out of a window over Greenland.

No one's saying Nine Iron tossed the poor fellow out, but Nine Iron did end up with the cabin. So draw your own conclusion.

It was a great trip and Nine Iron felt great, just great, as he stepped off the zeppelin in Rome, Italy.

Then he felt good taking a train to the seaside city of Naples.

And he felt okay taking the stagecoach to the small town of San Gudafella.

He felt slightly out of sorts riding a donkey up the side of Mount Vesuvius.

And by the time he reached the top, he was beginning to feel a bit nervous. Because first: he didn't like heights all that much. And, second: he didn't like being perched atop a rocky ridge above a vast sea of steaming hot magma.

His guide mutely pointed to a narrow pathway that

led down toward the magma. Then the guide turned his donkey around and took off.

Nine Iron set off down the inside of the caldera—the bowl of the volcano. The volcano was in a sort of constant low-key eruption. The volcano that back in Roman times had totally erupted and wiped out the city of Pompeii, burying everyone in ash and flying rock and a bit of lava. That volcano.

Down he climbed. Down and down and hotter and hotter until he could feel the heat coming up through his shoes.

And that's when Nine Iron saw his first monster. It looked like a giant bug wearing a striped suit and a fedora.

"I have come to—" the monster said.

Nine Iron shot him.

He stepped over the bug's body and kept going down the hill. He didn't know why the bug had talked to him, or what the bug was, but Nine Iron thought he looked like the kind of bug that, if smaller, would attack an oat crop.

And Nine Iron did not approve of oat pests.

He went on for another half hour; and this time

as he turned a blind corner, he was confronted by two fellows that might conceivably be human, except that they were very short, with stubby legs, and they were wearing lederhosen with an image of a tree on the front.

They each had a club and they smacked the clubs into their palms in a tough-guy manner. "Now listen, human slime—"

So Nine Iron shot them, too.

The next monster Nine Iron saw was just a leg. At least that's all he saw at first, because the leg itself from ankle to knee was about five feet. Then another five feet from knee to hip. And then about ten more feet from there to the neck.

The head was about twenty-five feet up.

Nine Iron shot this creature, too, but the creature didn't seem to notice. It reached down with one massive hand and lifted him up to examine him more closely.

The creature was covered with white fur that changed color as Nine Iron watched. It was ever so slightly pink.

Later Nine Iron would learn that this was a

Gudridan. And that you never wanted to see a pink Gudridan. And if you ever happened to see one gone full red, it would be the last thing you saw.

Some instinct warned Nine Iron that irritating the giant any further would be a bad thing. Probably it was the sight up close and stinky of the Gudridan's gaping mouth filled with large teeth.

"I have an appointment," Nine Iron said. "With the Pale Queen."

The giant said nothing. But a smaller creature, like a skinny dalmatian dog with a disfigured face and chewed-off fingers, said, "Yeah. So follow us."

Nine Iron jerked his head back up the trail. "Sorry about the others. . . ."

"Don't be stupid," the Lepercon snapped. "If you hadn't killed them, the Pale Queen would think you were soft."

"Ah," Nine Iron said. He thought about it for a second, then shot the Lepercon.

To the giant he said, "Okay, let's go."

Eighteen

Somehow—no one saw her move—Risky went from the mountaintop to the wall, just a base-ball throw away. She had the same deep red hair and the same scary, intense green eyes.

"I see you've found the dragon folk," Risky said. "Very nicely done, Mack. And you have this one"—she stabbed a finger at Jarrah—"to help guide you in the magic tongue."

"Say what?" Jarrah asked.

"Vargran," Risky explained. She seemed quite friendly. Maybe a little cocky, but no more arrogant or dangerous than any number of cheerleaders back at Mack's school. "And now the littlest dragon."

Risky's eyes grew colder as she contemplated Xiao. Xiao was still human in appearance. But obviously Ereskigal—aka Morgan le Fay and a host of other evildoers—was not easily tricked by appearances. "I really thought we'd finished the last of you off. But you had only found a nice hole to hide in. Now that we've found your hideaway beneath the Forbidden City, we'll come for your sorry race soon."

Xiao said, "I take from your words that your evil servants were repulsed from Dragon Home."

Risky smiled. "Oh, yes. It was a pretty one-sided battle. You dragons may not be fierce, but you do know how to summon the waters and make them do your bidding. So many Skirrit and Tong Elves died. Such a pity: all that tasty meat gone to waste. And I am really hungry."

"I can still do the burning thing!" Mack threatened.

"Yes," Risky admitted. "But you know it won't

work on me twice, right? Now. The question before us is: What's on the menu? Human meat? Dragon meat?"

Xiao slipped from her human mask and became the dragon once again. Then, without warning, she shot into the sky.

Mack was sure she would do something cool to Risky. Risky seemed a bit concerned herself, but Xiao rose, turned, and raced away along the wall.

She disappeared behind a mountain.

"Okay, then," Risky said. "Human meat it is."

"Run!" Mack yelled.

They ran in the same direction Xiao had taken. They leaped down elongated stairs.

"That's good," Risky called after them. "Get the blood flowing! It makes you more tender."

Mack risked a quick glance back at Risky, who was already beginning to change in rather dramatic ways. For one thing, wings were growing from her shoulders. For another thing, a new set of arms was protruding from her midriff.

And her green eyes were bulging, bulging, and becoming patterned in thousands of small hexagonal lenses. Like a dragonfly. In fact, exactly like a dragon-fly.

But bigger—like something the air force would build if it wanted a dragonfly to use in air-to-air combat.

They reached the closest tower and stopped inside, panting.

"I can't believe Xiao bailed on us!" Jarrah yelled.

"I would if I could," Mack said. He had a stitch in his side from running. He held it and doubled over.

"I don't think we're safe in here," Stefan said.

The tower wasn't that big, just as wide as the wall itself and extending up for maybe another fifty feet. It was brick and had been designed to be completely impervious. To arrows.

zzzz-ZZZZZ-zzzz-ZZZZZ

It was a whine like a fingernail scraping a single string on an electric guitar. Mack could see Risky through the arched, doorless opening. Her wings beat the air so fast they became nothing but a blur.

You could say she was a really big dragonfly, except that her face wasn't a dragonfly's face. It was still Risky, but all distended and distorted, as if someone had tried to stretch her face over a head ten sizes too big. Her lips were smeared into a wide Joker grin. The smile revealed curved, scimitar teeth that could be made of steel.

The six legs were no longer even slightly human. But they weren't quite insect, either. More like long, thin lobster claws.

"Aaah ahha yaarrgh!" the three of them said, more or less in unison.

"We need some Vargran!" Mack cried.

"Like what?" Jarrah yelled.

"Huh," Stefan said. "It's kind of cool the way she can do that."

"She's going to eat us!" Mack yelled at Stefan.

The dragonfly creature rose from the wall. For a few seconds Mack couldn't see her. But the drone sound came closer and louder, so loud he could hardly hear his own rasping breath.

She landed with a surprisingly small thump atop the tower. It barely shook the bricks.

She had managed what the swelling Lepercons could not do: she'd kept her weight in proportion. That, Mack reflected, was the key to getting really big:

you didn't want the weight going up proportionally.

But that didn't mean Risky wasn't strong. Mack heard a grinding, tearing noise and saw bricks falling outside. Risky was taking the tower apart, brick by brick.

There were a lot of bricks in the tower.

But not enough.

A beam of sunlight shone through a hole in the high, domed ceiling. One big, rainbow-shiny, multi-faceted eye stared down at them.

"I can hear your little hearts beating," Risky said. "Nothing's tastier than a fresh, frightened heart. Did you know it will keep beating for a while after I tear it from your chest, Mack? I'll feel it fluttering in my stomach."

"Vargran! We need some like, like, like right now!"

"I-I-I-I," Jarrah cried. "I can't think!"

Bricks fell down through the hole and landed around them.

Stefan snatched one up and hurled it at the big eye-ball. It missed.

With a ripping sound, the roof of the tower tore free. It lifted like a hinged lid. Then it collapsed and fell down the outside of the tower.

The tower was now a convertible with the top down.

Nothing was left to stop Risky. Nothing left but for her to decide who to eat first.

But suddenly Risky hesitated. Mack could see her creepy half-human, half-insect head snap up. It's hard to see fear in a face that . . . unusual . . . but Mack definitely heard concern in her voice.

"It can't be," Risky said. "I killed you a millennium ago!"

The biggest sound Mack had ever heard answered back. A voice so astounding that it was hard even to parse out the words. Which were:

"So long as the four winds blow, I live! I am Shen LOOOONG! And . . . I LIIIIIVE!"

Nineteen

When his insides had stopped quivering and his bones had stopped rattling from the sound, Mack turned and looked through the far door of the tower.

He was used to seeing dragons now. Well, kind of used to it. But this didn't look like the other dragons.

Shen Long had a face that seemed almost human. Maybe half dragon, half human. And at first he looked kind of comical, because he was less like a huge snake and more like a huge snake that had swallowed one of those domed telescope observatories.

His chest and stomach were bulbous, and vast.

He was sucking in air as if he was trying to get it all for himself. It was like standing in the surf when a wave recedes.

Xiao suddenly appeared and zoomed into the tower, knocking Mack flat in her hurry. "Down!" she yelled. "Down and hold on for dear life!"

Mack was already down. Stefan grabbed Jarrah and knocked her flat. The three of them were face-down, and Xiao was already zooming away when Shen Long finished filling his lungs.

Then, Shen Long exhaled.

The top three-quarters of the tower might as well have been a kid's papier-mâché art project. The hurricane, the tornado of wind, blew it away in a single piece.

Mack looked up in time to see Risky flying backward through the air. Not quite as fast as a bullet, maybe, but very fast.

She flew, helpless, in a maelstrom of bricks and chunks of tower and mismatched bits of crenellation.

She hit the next tower, smashed through it, hit the top of the wall beyond, rolled along the crenellations, came loose, flew some more, hit the top of a mountain, took the top of the mountain with her, and disappeared from view.

The hurricane ended as suddenly as it had begun.

Shen Long's stomach was still big. But not as big.

Xiao swept down from the sky and landed on his shoulder. "Uncle! Thanks!"

"Anything for my favorite niece," Shen Long said in a more subdued voice. "Besides, I can't stand that princess. She's as rotten as her mother."

"Is she dead?" Mack asked.

Xiao jumped in to do quick introductions.

"No, Mack, she's not dead. Not even killed," Shen Long said regretfully. "But it will take her a while to put herself back together. You'd better get going. She won't fall for the same thing twice."

"Actually, Uncle, I was wondering if you could give us a ride."

"A ride?" Shen Long scratched his chin with one five-clawed foot. "Where to?"

"Germany," Mack said. "Some place called the

Egge Rocks or Externsteine."

"Externsteine?" Shen Long looked troubled.

"Or the nearest airport," Mack said. "I know it's a long way."

Xiao, human once again, gave Mack a significant look. In a whisper she said, "The problem is not the distance. It's the memories."

Shen Long looked stricken. His jovial face was sad and creased with worry. He seemed to have decided what direction Germany was in and was staring that way, but with eyes that saw something else entirely.

"She wouldn't even remember me," Shen Long said softly.

"No one could ever forget you, Uncle. But it was a long time ago."

"I will take you," Shen Long said reluctantly. "But I am not hanging around. Otherwise she'll think I came to see her."

"As you wish, Uncle," Xiao said.

The dragon lay as flat as he could, and Xiao, followed by Mack, Jarrah, and Stefan, climbed up his side and onto his back. Like all Chinese dragons, he rose effortlessly, and headed away from the sun.

"What was all that about?" Mack asked. He was trying not to think about what would happen if he fell off. Shen Long was gaining altitude pretty quickly. Soon they were brushing the undersides of the clouds.

"An old love of my uncle's. Her name was Nott."

"Not what?"

"Nott. Just Nott."

Mack waited as long as he could before asking, "Not what?"

"Nott. That was her name. Nott."

"Is that a joke?" Mack asked. "Like one of those 'not' jokes? Like if I said, 'I like your dress . . . not.'"

"What's the matter with my dress?" Xiao asked, a little irritated.

Leaning forward, Jarrah asked, "Not what?"

"Not a what, a who," Mack explained to Jarrah. "Nothing!" he answered Xiao's question.

"Okay, then," Jarrah said. "Not who?"

"Are we there yet?" Stefan asked.

"I think Nott was Shen Long's girlfriend," Mack yelled back to Jarrah. The wind was fierce and cold now that Shen Long was picking up speed.

"Then what's this about nothing?" Jarrah asked.

"It's not about nothing," Mack said. "It's about Nott."

There was a moment or two of silence. Then Jarrah said, "You know, I could push you right off this dragon's back."

Mack thought that over for a second or two then said, "I'd prefer you not. Heh."

And so the first three of the Magnificent Twelve flew aboard a pot-bellied dragon into the west. And Stefan was there, too.

Mack leaned close to Stefan, not wanting the others to hear him. "Dude, we're cool, right?"

Stefan thought about that for a moment. "I'm cool. And Jarrah is definitely cool. So cool. But I'm not sure about you."

"That's not what I meant. I mean, you could have died. I probably should have gotten you to a doctor."

Stefan shrugged. "Why? I'm all fixed up."

"But I didn't know that at the time. I kind of risked your life."

Stefan laughed. "You're under my wing. Not the other way around." Then he punched Mack in the shoulder, one of those "friendly" punches. A buddy punch. Which knocked Mack clear off Shen Long's back and would have sent him spiraling down to plow a hole in some very hard-looking ground except that Stefan snatched him back and settled him in place again.

"See? Under my wing."

Twenty

They told knock-knock jokes over Mongolia.

They sang "Ninety-nine Bottles of Beer on the Wall" over Kazakhstan.

They stared blearily ahead with glazed, fixed expressions over Russia.

They stopped for water at a lake in Ukraine and used a porta-potty at an oil pipeline construction site.

They talked about their hopes and dreams and aspirations over Poland.

"I either want to be an extreme fighting champion," Stefan said, "or a race car driver."

"I want to be a surfer and go on the tour, you know?" Jarrah said. "Maybe get a sponsorship, right? Have lots of money but ride the big ones all day."

"Wouldn't that be boring after a while?" Mack asked.

"What, surfing? Boring?" Jarrah laughed like it was idiotic even to suggest such a thing. "Besides, I'd do a bit of archaeology in my spare time. Like my mum."

"What about you, Xiao?" Mack asked. He didn't like the conversation because he didn't want to answer the question for himself.

"I will be a dragon, of course," Xiao said.

"Yeah, okay, but aren't there different jobs for dragons? I mean, there must be, like . . . um . . . you know, dragon firefighters, dragon bus drivers. Maybe not bus drivers. But you know, different dragon jobs."

"We are born with certain duties," Xiao said. "We learn and we think and we write."

"Oh, please," Jarrah said with a derisive snort. "Don't give me all that good-girl, do-what-I'm-told stuff. No one wants to grow up to do just what

I HAVE MADE NEW FRIENDS IN DETENTION. THE FIRST DAY I MET MATTHEW AND HELDER AND DWAYNE.

SAID, "I ALWAYS KNEW YOU WERE CUTE, MACK. BUT I DIDN'T KNOW YOU WERE SO TOUGH." THEN SHE SAT NEXT TO ME.

AND I SAID "THANKS!" AGAIN. WE PLAYED THIS GAME UNTIL MATTHEW WAS TIRED. CAMARO, WHO IS A GIRL BULLY,

THEY ARE BULLIES. I THINK I SAT IN THE WRONG CHAIR, AND MATTHEW ASKED ME IF I WOULD LIKE HIM TO PUNCH ME IN THE HEAD. I SAID, "YES." BECAUSE IT'S IMPORTANT TO BE POSITIVE. MATTHEW PUNCHED ME AND I THANKED HIM. SO HE PUNCHED ME AGAIN their parents tell them."

Xiao sighed. Mack was sure she was going to stick to her previous statement. But then she said, "The truth is, I love playing sports. At the school, we sometimes play football or basketball. I love basketball."

"You play hoops?"

"I like being part of a team. It is a very human experience, you know. We—we dragons—are solitary. We don't have teams. Handing the ball to someone else so that the team will prosper, it is a new challenge. The idea that the individual must sacrifice for the common good, that is very dragonlike. But doing this within a team, as a strategy for victory, that is new."

"So you want to be either a dragon or a basketball star?" Jarrah didn't sound skeptical. In fact, she obviously liked the idea.

Xiao laughed. "I can't help but be a dragon. But when I daydream, in the hour before sleep, I sometimes picture myself as part of China's Olympic team."

"Are your parents okay with that?" Mack asked.

"No," Xiao said, sounding annoyed. Then, in a more resigned tone, she repeated, "No."

"Do you know kung fu?" Stefan called up to her.

"You could give me lessons."

Xiao turned her head as far around as she could and stared at Stefan. "No. No, I do not know kung fu."

Stefan blushed.

"What about you, Mack?" Jarrah asked. "What are you going to be when you grow up?"

"We're almost there, probably," Mack deflected.

"You're deflecting," Jarrah said. "Come on, we all told."

"Chef," Mack said.

"What?"

"A chef. Okay? I want to be a chef when I grow up." Then he added, "If I grow up. Which is seeming less and less likely."

"That's like a cook, right?" Jarrah asked.

"Kind of," Mack said. It was embarrassing to him to talk about this. He was twelve. Twelve-year-old boys were supposed to want to be cops or firefighters or soldiers or wizards or at least game designers or billionaires. Not chefs.

But at the formative age of three, Mack had watched his father putting ingredients into the blender as he made a so-called health shake. Strawberries, okay.

Banana, okay. Yogurt, sure. But even at the tender age of three, Mack had known the raw potatoes were a mistake.

Since then, Mack had become a student of his parents' cooking. His father had a habit of odd substitutions. ("No," Mack would say, "you can't substitute American cheese for butter in a cake; it won't work.") And his mother tended to cook foods until they were not only done, not only overdone, but reduced to a flavorless gray goo you could suck up through a straw. (Brussels sprouts are bad enough—liquid brussels sprouts are even worse.)

As Mack had grown, he'd experienced much bad cooking. But then, one day, his parents had taken him to a dress-up restaurant to celebrate his mother's promotion. The restaurant had a white tablecloth and crystal glasses. And the food! Baby vegetables cooked just right. A piece of fish that was not a stick or a patty or a cake. Just fish! And a dessert that was neither Costco ice cream nor Sam's Club cookies.

It had opened Mack's eyes. Since that day he'd wanted to wear the toque, learn to cook, become a chef.

Now, he reflected, he was stuck in a very different "job." He was riding on the back of a dragon. Not quite what he'd dreamed about.

"I'm riding on a dragon," Mack said out loud.

"Yeah. Cool, huh?" Jarrah said.

"This is what I do now," he said. "I ride dragons and fight monsters."

"And save the world," Jarrah said.

"It is an honor," Xiao offered.

"It's a kick," Jarrah said.

"Huh," Stefan said.

"We are near the spot," Shen Long said.

Mack looked down and saw mountains. And a lake. And a lot of trees. The sun rose behind them and cast a delicate gray-pink light.

Shen Long circled the place slowly. "I remember this place," he said. "I know what is here."

"What is here, Uncle?" Xiao asked gently.

"Help for you in your quest, I hope," Shen Long said. "But only painful memories for me."

"If you saw her again . . ."

"No," the big dragon said, and shook his head. "Old wounds are best left alone." Then his tone of voice changed. "And new wounds are best avoided."

Mack was looking at the ground, so Jarrah spotted the problem before he did: two jets painted in dark green camouflage inscribing a shockingly fast turn across the blue sky.

"It's this newfangled radar thing," Shen Long said tersely. "I really don't approve."

"The Pale Queen has fighter jets?" Jarrah cried.

"I don't know," Mack said. "But the German air force does."

"We have to land," Shen Long said. "There's a town ahead. Hold on tight!"

The dragon dived toward the ground. The trees rushed up toward them as the two Eurofighter jets roared overhead.

Shen Long landed at a gas station—it was early, so the station was closed—and Mack and his friends quickly climbed down.

"May fortune smile upon you," Shen Long said, and rose from the ground.

"They'll blast you out of the air!" Jarrah cried.

"I command the winds, child," Shen Long said. "No missile will harm me."

Mack walked around to look Shen Long more or less in the face. "Thanks, um, sir, for the ride." He wasn't quite sure if "sir" was what you called a dragon.

"No, youngster, thank you," Shen Long said. "You have undertaken a dangerous task. You face almost certain death."

"I do?"

"You all do," Shen Long said. "Do you not know the fate of the original Magnificent Twelve?"

"Um . . . I know Grimluk's looking kind of grody."

"Of the Twelve, very few survived the battle with the Pale Queen."

"Ah."

"And those who made it were taken one at a time in battle chasing her foul daughter. Until only Grimluk survived. And he is alive only because his hiding place is unknown to all."

"Sounds a bit grim then, eh?" Jarrah said cheerfully.

Xiao came and sort of hugged the dragon. Shen Long said, "Be careful, Niece. Those you go to see were quick to anger in their youth. And if you happen to see . . ." He trailed off.

"If I see Nott, I will tell her that you remember her

with great fondness."

The dragon tilted his massive head, a little embarrassed. "Just say . . . Yes, as you said. Great fondness. But don't make me seem desperate."

"Of course not."

"Or needy."

"Absolutely."

"And don't set anything up."

They watched him go up, up into the sky. Mack still had a hard time believing something that big and that pot-bellied could fly. Of course, he reflected, the poor fighter pilots would have an even harder time believing it. On radar Shen Long would have just looked like an unknown plane.

"Now what?" Jarrah asked.

"Breakfast," Stefan said.

Twenty-one

DID WE MENTION IT'S A LONG TIME AGO?

Paddy—newly remonikered as Nine Iron—Trout was wondering just how much farther down they had to go. Already the Gudridan had led him so far down that the edge of the volcano's bowl towered so high above him he felt like he was at the bottom of a well.

It was getting warmer. And the air smelled less

and less like air and more and more like someone had bought a lot of expired eggs and then fried them up with some rancid goat meat.

The lava bubbled in sullen pools not thirty feet below them. One wrong step on the narrow path would plunge Nine Iron to his death. There was no guardrail. There wasn't even a warning sign.

To make matters worse, the Gudridan walked very quickly—as you might expect from a creature with legs that long—and Nine Iron had to trot to keep up.

Suddenly the Gudridan stopped. Nine Iron looked around, baffled. The path just ended. Sheer rock wall to the left, sheer fall into percolating magma on the other side. And the path, which had only been maybe four feet wide to begin with, suddenly narrowed to inches and then to nothing at all.

"Here," the Gudridan said.

"Where?"

The Sasquatch-looking creature pointed at a circle cut into the rock. It was right around chest level for Nine Iron. Words in an alphabet he didn't recognize were chiseled in a ring around the circle.

"Is that supposed to be a doorbell?"

The Gudridan shrugged. Clearly he was not going to be helpful. So Nine Iron pushed against the inset circle. The rock gave way, and Nine Iron was just congratulating himself on having gotten it right when his hand plunged in way, way too far.

The circle was no longer a circle; it was a mouth ringed with very sharp, curved teeth. The teeth bit down just enough to keep Nine Iron from pulling his hand back out.

When Nine Iron peered into the hole, past the ring o' teeth, he saw what looked like a pulsating red tube.

"Hey!" Nine Iron yelled.

The Gudridan smiled cruelly. "Pay the blood price."

"Pay the what now?"

"The Mother of All Monsters wants a taste."

"A taste of . . . ?"

"Blood."

That was really not the answer Nine Iron had been hoping for. On the other hand, he respected irrational bloodthirstiness as a character trait. (How could he not?)

He took a deep breath and began to pull his hand

out. The teeth never clamped down, but they never withdrew, either, so as he pulled his hand away, the teeth cut shallow but still painful grooves in his skin.

More disturbing than the pain was the fact that as the blood ran in streams from his hand, the red tube began sucking, sucking hard. Like a kid with a milkshake and a narrow straw.

Nine Iron drew his hand all the way out, leaving behind a bit of skin and a bit of blood.

"Next time don't ring the bell," the Gudridan suggested. "Just knock."

The stone wall that had seemed so stonelike just seconds before now grew soft and pulpy. Like stone-colored flesh rather than stone-colored stone.

Then an X appeared in the middle of this fleshy panel. The X grew, and each triangle became a sharp tongue. The four tongues then thrust out, and Nine Iron was confronted with one of the more unusual entryways he'd ever see.

He had to step on the bottom tongue to go through. It was spongy beneath his feet, and so hot he could feel it through the soles of his shoes.

He stepped into a tunnel that was not at all what

he expected. No musty old boulders, no stalactites or stalagmites. No park ranger tour guide or souvenir shop.

The tunnel was twenty feet in diameter, and it was as alive and fleshy and moist as the sharp-tongued entryway. He was not in a cave; he was inside something alive.

The "door" closed behind him with a sound like smacking lips. The Gudridan had not come inside after him.

Nine Iron was a tough guy. But he was starting to get just the slightest bit nervous. Something about being inside a living thing was unnerving. But he walked steadily forward down the pulpy, red-glowing, gently pulsating tunnel. Because judging from what he'd seen so far, whimpering and begging to be let go probably wasn't going to work. And there wasn't much he could really shoot.

He walked for two minutes at a steady pace, and then noticed that the "floor" was sloping upward. The tunnel was coated with a viscous goo—not too thick, but enough that it made things slippery—so going uphill was not easy. Nine Iron wished hiking boots had been invented since those would be more helpful than the slick-soled Goochies he was wearing.

Soon he was on hands and knees, slipping and sliding and cursing freely as he made his way up the slope. Then, quite suddenly, he reached the end.

The tube or tunnel, or whatever it was, opened onto a sort of cavern the color of liver. In fact it might have been a liver: the only anatomy Nine Iron knew was the best places to stab someone. (His Nafia education was a bit one-dimensional.)

This chamber was a sort of massive eggplant shape with dozens of openings similar to the one in which Nine Iron now stood.

The bottom of the eggplant chamber was a membrane, like the skin of a drum. Tendrils rose like living stalactites or stalagmites (depending on which is the one that goes up) and they made a sort of forest like something you'd see on the floor of the ocean.

Suddenly what looked like a very large wad of mucus (we try to avoid words like *snot*) came shooting from one of the tubes. It was followed quickly by two more. The wads—each the size of a boxing heavy bag, the color and consistency of a spit-saturated cigar, and coated with what you get if you leave chewed gum out in the sun—plopped onto the membrane.

There the stalactendrils seized each pellet and began sucking away the goo. This eventually, after way too much straw-sucking-on-the-last-of-a-milkshake noise, revealed three insectoid creatures like the one Nine Iron had shot on the pathway.

They didn't seem to notice him but, once freed of encumbrance, began searching for the right tube. This involved counting on their fingers (not exactly base ten, as you can imagine) and then counting off tunnels. Finally they seemed to agree on the right tube, scampered up the slick side of the chamber, and slid into it.

Nine Iron was somewhat at a loss how to react to this. But he didn't have to wait long, for now his eyes were drawn irresistibly to the prettiest girl Nine Iron had ever seen. She had an amazing amount of wavy red hair, skin so pale it was practically see-through, and eyes like emeralds. She walked through the sea of stalactendrils like one of those impossibly pretty girls who are always walking through fields of flowers in TV commercials for pharmaceutical products that turn out to cause oily discharge or make your hair fall out.

Of course TV had only recently been invented, so they didn't have TV commercials for dangerous pharmaceuticals that cause oily discharge and hair loss yet. So Nine Iron could only note that she was quite an attractive girl.

Quite . . . attractive.

"Hi; you would be Paddy Trout," the girl said.

She smiled engagingly so that Nine Iron thought he might just ask her out to a nice oat-gruel dinner. Then afterward they could attend a bearbaiting, or a bare-knuckle prize fight, or even, if she played her cards right, a cockfight.

"I'm Risky," she said.

Nine Iron leered and said, "Risky, eh? I'll bet—"

And right then he noticed that he couldn't breathe. At all. Like something was choking him.

And then he noticed that the something was a snake that seemed to form from Risky's long, luscious red hair.

Because that's the kind of thing you notice.

Risky's lovely face was close to his. "You were about to say, 'I'll bet you are,'" Risky said, still very pleasant—aside from the choking-hair thing. "I hate that joke."

Nine Iron managed to grunt in a way that might have been "Sorry."

The hair snake withdrew, and Nine Iron sucked fetid oxygen.

"You're here to meet my mother," Risky said.

Nine Iron nodded and croaked the words "Pale Queen" through his crushed windpipe.

"Follow me. But watch the jokes: Mom has, like, no sense of humor."

Twenty-two

Do you ever find yourself in a place you never thought you'd be? A place that doesn't seem to make any sense within the narrative of your life? And you get this kind of queasy, "whoa, life is kind of weird and unpredictable" feeling? And you start wondering if this is the start of some long spiral into complete strangeness? Even madness?

You might expect Mack to have gotten that feeling when he was chased out of his school by Skirrit, or when he was down inside of Uluru, or maybe when he was being chased around the Donghuamen Night Market by elves on bikes.

But for some reason the weirdness struck him now.

He was sitting at a square wooden table that was partly covered with a white cloth. Him, Jarrah, Stefan, and Xiao. On the table were cups filled with painfully hot chocolate and plates displaying the remains of their ravaged meal.

A few feet away was the breakfast buffet table, loaded down with bread and cold cuts and cheese and yogurt and some gravel-looking granola, and canned pineapple.

There was a wire bowl that had contained chubby little donuts—they'd all been eaten, leaving behind a light crust of sugar crystals on all four mouths.

They were still working on bread and butter and lingonberry jam, eating like people whose last meal had been scorpions on a stick.

It was the dining room of a hotel in Detmold, Germany. Not exactly the weirdest place Mack had been recently. In fact, it was so very close to normal that it seemed especially strange.

Sometimes all-out weird feels less weird than something just slightly off center.

Anyway, they were having breakfast, cautiously sipping hot chocolate, incautiously slathering butter onto bread, and asking each other politely to pass the jam.

Detmold was a pleasant little town with a lot of buildings in the Gothic timber-framed look you've seen in every movie about Martin Luther or Joan of Arc. (And surely you've seen a few of those.)

Basically you imagine taking some Lincoln Logs, making a sort of loose framework for a three- or four-story building. Then you imagine using white Play-Doh to fill in all the rectangles and triangles between the logs. Slap on a high, peaked roof covered in depressing gray tiles, stick in some windows with lots of tiny frames, and you have the idea.

Now, since this is modern Germany, not Detmold the way it was back in, oh, let's say the fourteenth century (when people were dying from the plague and eating rats and anxiously awaiting the invention of the shower), you have to picture some shiny Mercedeses and Audis parked here and there. And some more modern buildings. In fact, mostly more modern buildings, but why confuse things?

For Mack's purposes, the important thing about Detmold was that the Detmoldians made a decent cup of cocoa.

After they finished their breakfast and Mack had paid with the special Magnificent 12 credit card, he took out his phone, punched up the map, and said, "I think it's that way," and pointed.

The "it" in question was the  Externsteine. The Egge Rocks, as Grimluk had called them.

They began to walk. It was several miles away, but the air wasn't cold, and the sun was shrouded behind thin clouds and just barely above the horizon anyway, so it was pleasant enough walking weather. Besides, none of them could read German, so the bus stops they passed were indecipherable.

Soon after leaving the town, however, they found themselves walking into fog. Very thick fog, in fact. It didn't seem that sticking to the road would be too hard, but it was a bit nerve-racking because cars continued to pass by. It seemed to Mack that walking on the shoulder of the road in close to zero visibility was an excellent way to get run over by a Volkswagen.

But there wasn't much they could do about it. And after a while of practically feeling their way through the fog, Mack realized they hadn't seen a car for some time.

"Ow!" Jarrah yelled.

Mack could barely make her out even though she was just a few feet away. "What's the matter?"

"Nothing. I just walked into a sign and banged my knee."

Mack went toward her and now he, too, could see the sign. "Freilichtmuseum," Mack read. "What's that?"

"A museum for freilichts?" Jarrah suggested.

"So, no idea?"

"Not a clue, mate."

Mack carefully typed the word into the browser on his phone. "It's an open-air museum."

"Okay."

He checked the map app. "I think we're off the road a little. Stefan! Xiao!"

They managed to find one another by calling out.

And now the fog was thinning just a bit. And yet it seemed colder. They were in what looked very much like a medieval village. An empty medieval village.

"I think it's maybe like a German Williamsburg, you know?" Mack said, squinting to read his browser. "People dress up all medieval and show you how to shoe a horse or make candles or whatever."

"There's no one here," Stefan said.

"Actually, there are people in that hut there." Xiao pointed. Mack saw a couple of men dressed in leather breeches and loose-fitting shirts.

"I don't see anyone," Stefan said.

Just then a man came pushing past carrying a rough-hewn cage filled with rats.

"I hate rats," Mack said.

"Me, too," Stefan agreed. "But I don't see any rats."

"In that guy's cage," Mack said.

"What guy?"

Mack stopped walking. "Xiao? Jarrah? You saw the guy with the box of rats, right?"

Both said they had. Stefan had not.

Nor did Stefan see the woman leading a cow.

Nor did he see the two men laboring to lift bundles

of firewood into a wagon. Or the young girl carrying a baby. Or the fat old bald guy riding backward on a horse.

In a few more seconds of increasingly perplexed and then panicky conversation, it became clear that Stefan was seeing something entirely different from what they were seeing.

Stefan saw a completely empty, but neat and well-preserved, assemblage of old buildings—a village with a large windmill.

The rest of them saw a scattering of lean-tos and barely standing shacks and a population of young, very dirty, rag-bedecked people with few teeth and no sense of style or standards of personal grooming.

The young girl carrying the baby was joined by a young man—in fact he might be no older than twelve or so—leading a pair of cows.

"You don't see that?" Mack pressed.

"No. No, I don't see cows or a baby or some dude," Stefan maintained.

"He does not possess the *enlightened puissance*," a voice said in German-accented English.

Mack spun around and there, emerging from the fog, was a boy. He had on jeans and a denim jacket.

He might have looked tough, except that he didn't. He was painfully thin, tallish, with fine blond hair down to his shoulders. He had a soft mouth and big brown eyes. Mack thought he looked about ten years old.

"I am Dietmar," the boy said.

"Good for you," Stefan snapped. "Now what was that you called me?"

"You do not see what they see," Dietmar said in a low, reverential voice. "For they possess the *enlightened puissance*. They are of the Magnifica."

"And what is it you see?" Mack demanded, only slightly less hostile than Stefan. The rats had unsettled him. That plus the feeling that maybe he was hallucinating.

"I see what you see," Dietmar said. "I see Gelidberry and her husband fleeing their village as the Pale Queen approaches."

Mack froze.

The boy made his quick, short-duration smile. "You know his name, surely? That young man who flees?"

Mack watched the couple with the baby and the two cows walking quickly away.

"Grimluk," Mack whispered.

Twenty-three

"Okay, what is this, some kind of trick?" Jarrah demanded. The notion made her angry.

Dietmar shook his head. "This is a very old site. Long before the Freilichtmuseum was built, or the medieval village, there was an earlier village in this place. Long, long ago."

"Three thousand years," Mack said.

"Yes," Dietmar agreed. "This is a place of power. Very few can even feel it, and only one with the *enlightened puissance* can see through the mist of time."

The fog was clearing now. Warmth returned as the sun peeked through. Now they all saw the restored village as others saw it, as an outdoor museum. Gone were the phantasms of an earlier age.

"If you saw it, then you must be one of us," Xiao said to Dietmar.

"One of the Magnificent Twelve?" Dietmar nodded. "Yes. I am Dietmar Augestein."

He extended a hand, and Jarrah shook it. Then she made a wry face. "Might want to put a little more gristle in that handshake there, mate."

Dietmar didn't seem to know what to make of that.

For his part, Mack wasn't quite sure what to make of this boy, or of this encounter. He had been strangely moved by the vision—hallucination, whatever it was—of Grimluk as a youth. Had Grimluk caused the apparition? Was this Grimluk reaching out to say, "See, I was young once, too, and scared"?

"Did someone tell you to meet us?" Mack asked.

Dietmar blushed. It was very visible because his skin was extremely pale and the blush crept up his neck like a rising tide.

"Not a person. In my family's *schloss* there are ancient rooms, down under the ground."

"*Schloss?*"

"It's like a castle." He shrugged. "Perhaps you don't believe me."

"You'd be amazed what we'll believe," Mack said.

"This castle is not so old, but before this castle was another, and another before that, you see? Each one built atop the last. Just like this village. But if you know the way, you can find the ancient rooms. I love this, to look at ancient things."

"Is this a long story?" Mack interrupted.

"Yes."

"I don't mean to be rude," Mack said. "But it seems like everywhere we go, someone shows up and tries to kill us. So just tell me the quick version."

"I am the great, great, great, great, great, great, great, great, great, great, great—"

"Quicker than that."

"Great-one-hundred-forty-nine-times-in-all–grandson of Grimluk and Gelidberry." Dietmar frowned. "I don't expect you to believe me, but you must. I know it seems incredible."

"Incredible? Not really," Mack said. "Last night a giant grasshopper tried to kill me, I was smacked by an elf, attacked by a shape-shifting death princess on the Great Wall of China, and I rode here on the back of a lovesick dragon."

"I see," Dietmar said.

"You see?" Mack echoed.

"All of this that seems so strange to you seems less strange to me," Dietmar said. "I have long known of the *enlightened puissance* and its uses. When you perhaps spent your time in playing video games, I read ancient texts in forgotten languages."

"What exactly is the *enlightened puissance*? That's something I'd actually love to know," Mack said, weary and feeling that Dietmar was a bit pedantic. So pedantic, in fact, that he probably knew just what *pedantic* meant without having to look it up. (Let's save you the trouble. Some synonyms for *pedantic*: precise, exact, perfectionistic, punctilious, and quibbling.)

"The *enlightened puissance* is a sort of capability, a talent, you might say," Dietmar lectured. "It is like electricity in that it powers other things: language, for example, or sight."

"Yeah, it's why we can use Vargran and most people can't," Jarrah said.

"Exactly," Dietmar said. "But it is not an infinite power source. It is like a battery: if you use it too much, it weakens, and then it must be recharged."

Mack narrowed his eyes. He was trying to decide whether Dietmar really knew a lot or was just acting like he did. "You mean it may suddenly fade out when we need it?"

Dietmar nodded. "Perhaps that is why there must be twelve Magnifica and not three or nine."

"Or five," Stefan guessed.

Dietmar said, "I think that's implied."

"How about four?" Stefan said.

"The *enlightened puissance* has a different frequency for each of us. At least that is what I believe, based on my reading."

"Yeah, the reading you did while we were all playing games," Mack said.

"Exactly," Dietmar said, apparently not getting that Mack was being just a wee bit snarky. "We may find we each have specialties, things we can do that others of the twelve cannot."

"Is your superpower talking a lot?" Stefan grumbled.

"It is a long walk from here to the Externsteine," Dietmar said, pointedly ignoring Stefan. "Eight kilometers." So as they walked through the outdoor museum, then out into the immaculate and manicured countryside, Mack heard the long version of Dietmar's story, which we don't need to inflict on ourselves right now. Suffice it to say a great deal had happened to Dietmar's family in the last three thousand years. Lots of moving around, lots of begetting, some Huns, some Tartars, approximately eight hundred ninety-four wars, and finally up to the point where Dietmar began nosing around the sub-sub-subbasements of his family's *schloss* and discovered their long, long, long history.

Dietmar was into details—exact details—so mostly Mack zoned out and looked around. There were woods coming up on the right. Dark woods.

"So what made you decide we would be here?" Mack asked.

"I thought you would be at the Externsteine, actually. But when I saw the fog, and saw that it was centered on the old village, I knew you were being guided there. It is not my first vision of the old ones." Dietmar sighed. "I know that this is the year in which the Pale Queen rises. And I believed—or maybe I only hoped—that I was to be one of the Magnificent Twelve."

"But why today?"

"I have ridden my bicycle out to the Externsteine every day since I learned that I possessed the *enlightened puissance* and perhaps was to be part of the Magnificent Twelve. Seventy-two days. Each day I rode my bicycle before school. And then after school I would go back."

Just then Mack's phone made a tinkly sound announcing a new message. He looked at the screen.

> Camaro says I must dance. (smiley face) Your golem.

Camaro could only be Camaro Angianelli, the official bully of geeks back at Richard Gere Middle School. (Go, Fighting Pupfish!)

Mack had never heard of making kids dance, but maybe she was tired of purple nurples, swirlies, thumbtacking, pantsing, tripping, headlocking, and good old-fashioned punching. He could easily picture Camaro forcing a geek to dance.

More interesting to Mack was the fact that the golem had somehow been classified as a geek.

He texted back:

If Camaro says dance, just dance. Do your best.

"So you felt the call of destiny," Jarrah was saying to Dietmar.

"Not really."

"You wished to honor your ancestors, Grimluk and Gelidberry?" Xiao suggested.

Dietmar looked a little uncomfortable. As if destiny and ancestors were alien concepts. "I just believed from what I had read that the Magnificent Twelve would arise. And that they would come to the Externsteine. Sooner or later." He shrugged. "I simply believed I was right."

"Why the Externsteine? Why would Grimluk send us here?" Mack asked. But just then a big bus came rushing by.

"Tourists," Dietmar said. "Come to see the Externsteine. We will not be alone."

Mack watched the bus barrel away, then slow to turn in. He stared after it. No. No way. No way Nine Iron could have gotten on a plane and made it here this quickly.

"Did anyone else see a green hat go flashing by on that bus?" asked Mack.

"Xiao. You might want to go airborne and see what's ahead," Mack said. Then he stopped himself. "Not that I'm trying to tell you what to do."

Xiao gave the matter some consideration. "Since you are the first of the Magnificent Twelve, you are the elder. Like an elder brother. We should do as you say."

"Only as long as he doesn't get bossy," Jarrah said.

"Only if he is right," Dietmar said.

For his part, Mack felt maybe they should have an election to decide who was in charge. But there wasn't exactly time for that. In any case, Xiao had already transformed.

Dietmar hadn't seen this happen before. "This is not possible."

Mack and Jarrah shared a grin.

Dietmar shook his head. "No, this is definitely not

possible. Laws of physics are being violated."

Xiao refused to be stopped by mere laws of physics and writhed up into the sky. She was back a minute later.

"I saw the rocks, the Externsteine. They are magnificent in a sort of crude way. I also saw the bus and people getting off. They looked like regular tourists. But there was a very old man in green."

"How did he get here so fast? He would have had to go straight from the Forbidden City to the airport."

"Private plane?" Jarrah suggested.

"I don't know," Mack admitted. "I'm just saying that for a very slow guy, he gets around pretty fast."

"Let's go," Stefan said grimly. "I owe Paddy Wacky."

Mack fretted. "I wish I knew what we're supposed to do when we get to these stupid rocks. I mean, this is not about fighting Nine Iron."

"What are your instructions?" Dietmar asked reasonably.

Mack threw his hands up. "We don't have real clear instructions. Grimluk sent me to Beijing, where we met Xiao. After that, all we had was something about the Egge Rocks and an ice show."

"Eyes show?" Dietmar said.

Mack looked at him thoughtfully. "You know what? Maybe it was *eyes*. That would make more sense than *ice*."

"We're magnificent, not necessarily brilliant," Jarrah said.

"Then it is good you have me because I am brilliant," Dietmar said. He did not say it as a joke. "My family name is Augestein. Most people think it is from Augustus, the Roman emperor."

"Yeah, I was going to guess that," Jarrah said dryly.

"But in fact *Auge* is the word for *eye*."

"And *Stein* is the word for *beer glass*," Stefan said.

"Actually it is the word for *stone*."

"Then why does my uncle Fritz always say, 'Draw me a stein of Yuengling from the keg in the basement'?"

"The 'ice show' is actually the 'eyes show.'" Mack looked at Dietmar more carefully. He hadn't taken to Dietmar at first. Neither had Jarrah, obviously. The casual mention of an ancient castle and the talk about being descended from Grimluk himself had seemed like showing off. Mack didn't like people who thought they were better than other people. Jarrah liked them even less. Only Xiao seemed indifferent—maybe she thought all nondragons were more or less the same.

"Augestein. The eyes. The 'eyes show,'" Mack repeated. "Grimluk was sending us to meet you. So that the eyes—the *Auge*, you—could show us the Egge Rocks. The Externsteine."

"That makes sense," Dietmar said.

"Seriously? That makes sense to you? He couldn't have just said, 'Go find this kid named Dietmar; he'll take you to the Externsteine'?"

Dietmar shrugged. "The important thing is that you found me. And now I will take you to the Egge Rocks, the Externsteine."

Dietmar was seriously irritating Mack with his attitude. Also his long blond hair, which girls would probably really like. But Dietmar was one of them, like him or not. And Mack realized he might not like a lot of the Twelve. But liking wasn't important. All that mattered was staying alive and not letting the Pale Queen win.

"Well, Dietmar Augestein, what are we supposed to do? What are we supposed to discover now that we're at the Externsteine?"

Dietmar looked nonplussed. "I don't know."

"I know exactly what to do," Stefan said. "Kick that old man's butt."

He plunged straight into the narrow band of woods that separated them from the Externsteine.

"But we don't have a plan," Dietmar protested.

"We never do, really," Jarrah said. "Come on, your lordship, I believe we're going to have a good old fight."

They emerged from the woods into a lovely, park-like setting. A well-tended lawn bordered a small lake shaped like a mirror image of the state of Vermont.

The Externsteine itself was a series of tall rock pillars. Maybe a couple hundred feet tall. They were light in color, devoid of trees or grass—just giant rock fingers thrust into the air.

Mack's first impression was that they looked like a small surviving part of some bigger structure. Like an architectural ruin, a segment of the walls of Troy, or a slice from a Mayan pyramid.

Imagine a row of those giant smokestacks you see sticking up out of power plants. Now imagine they're white. And then imagine they're all cracked and crumbly.

And you're standing right where it would all

crack and crumble down.

They looked broken. Worn by time. They cast very long shadows in the early, slanting sun. It was in the pattern of those shadows that Mack could see that the pillars were in roughly ascending heights, with the tallest pillar right up against, and even somewhat in, the lake.

The lake was nothing special—a pond, really. The water was dark and cloudy green.

"This is an ancient place," Xiao said. "I feel long memories touching this place. Strangeness. Danger. Evil. But faith and hope, too."

"It has a certain Uluruness about it," Jarrah admitted.

"There are stairs climbing up. A walkway. Do we go?" Xiao asked.

Nine Iron stood between them and the start of the ascending path. Tourists from the bus were unlimbering their cameras, stretching, looking around anxiously for a restroom.

"I don't see any Lepercons," Mack said. "And if we run—or even walk quickly—we can get around Nine Iron."

Stefan, however, was not interested in getting around Nine Iron. He strode with manly purpose straight toward the ancient man in green.

"You and me, old man," Stefan said.

Nine Iron grinned wickedly with his unhealthy horse teeth and his pale, bloodless lips. He slowly drew his cane-sword.

Stefan waited. "First thing I'm going to do is shove that cane right up your—"

And that's when someone stepped out from behind Nine Iron.

He couldn't be more than twelve. He was a small-ish kid. He had skin the color of caramel, big dark eyes, long black hair with lots of body, tied in a thick ponytail.

He was dressed in loose-fitting, even billowy white trousers. His shirt was a close-fitting embroidered jacket of a strange pinkish, salmonish color.

Around his waist was a green satin sash. Two jeweled scabbards were stuck into that sash. And in his hand was a staff maybe five feet long.

This rather incredible-looking boy twirled the staff in one hand with practiced ease.

Nine Iron said, "May I present my apprentice."

"Valin," the boy said. And he bowed from the waist, just a slight inclination, and an arrogant one at that. He smirked at Mack, ignoring Stefan.

"Step off, kid," Stefan warned.

Valin laughed delightedly. "I am well-versed in all manner of combat, mayhem, brawling, and assassination."

"Good for you," Stefan said. He reached to shove the boy aside.

That's when the stick whirled in Valin's hand and knocked Stefan's hand aside, spun, smacked Stefan in the side of the head, and ended by jabbing at Stefan's stomach.

Stefan landed flat on his behind, but he was up in the blink of an eye.

"Little weird dude, stay out of my way," Stefan warned. "Or I might kill you by accident."

"That would be a very . . . ," Nine Iron began. *Wheeze. Wheeze.* ". . . bad idea. You see, my apprentice here is one of you."

"It's true," Valin said. "I, too, have the *enlightened puissance.* But unlike you hopeless fools, I serve the Pale Queen."

Twenty-four

"What?" Mack said.

"You can't be on her side!" Jarrah cried.

"That is cheating!" Dietmar cried.

Valin shrugged. "If you kill me, you will never assemble the full Magnificent Twelve. And if you don't kill me, then I will kill you."

"Wait a minute," Mack said. "You're twelve and you're already evil? That's impossible!"

"Really?" Valin asked smugly. "Think about it."

So Mack did think about it. And when he thought

back over the many twelve-year-olds he knew or had known, he was a lot less sure that none of them were evil. Still, actually working for the Pale Queen and being an apprentice to a Nafia assassin seemed a little much. He said so.

Mack was stalling. First because it seemed crazy, even by the new and lower standards of crazy he had come to accept. He wanted some explanation.

But he was also stalling because Stefan was edging away unnoticed by the arrogant and flamboyantly attired stranger. It was absolutely impossible that Stefan would be fleeing, which could only mean that Stefan was up to something.

"Did you have, like, a bad childhood or something?" Mack pressed.

Valin made a phony sad face and said, "It's been a hard life for me. Boo-hoo."

"Maybe we could get you some counseling."

Valin's smirk evaporated. "You know nothing, fool. You don't know who I am. Or where I come from. Or why it is that I must destroy you."

"I've got some free time," Mack said. "You could tell me all about it."

"I think not," the boy said. "I will only say that

when I have destroyed you, my family will be avenged for an ancient injustice done to us by your family."

"I don't think my mom and dad ever—" Mack began.

"He's stalling," Nine Iron broke in. "Take him, my young apprentice!"

Mack figured he only needed another few seconds. He figured this because, as always, he noticed things. And the thing he had noticed was that the tour bus's engine had just roared to life. And he had a pretty good idea who was sitting behind the wheel.

"Stalling? Me? I just have an interest in history," Mack said. It was a statement that would have caused his history teacher at Richard Gere Middle School (Go, Fighting Pupfish!) to laugh and laugh and then start weeping.

There came the grinding of gears, and the bus came wallowing up over the lawn.

Nine Iron spun toward the bus with his usual cat-like speed—if the cat you're talking about is a dead one. But Valin was much quicker. He grabbed his ancient master and threw him to the ground.

The bus swept over them both.

Stefan hit the brakes, and the bus stopped with

both Nine Iron and Valin beneath it.

"Go go go!" Mack yelled.

He, Dietmar, Jarrah, and Xiao raced for the path up onto the Externsteine. Stefan brought up the rear.

It took a while for Valin to extricate Nine Iron from under the bus. He had to crawl back under to retrieve his master's cane-sword. Then he had to wait for Nine Iron to gasp, wheeze, cough, pant, gargle a little phlegm, and take a good spit. And by then the Magnificent Four were pushing past slow-moving tourists and racing up stone steps and across rickety, rusted steel arches, from stone to stone, toward the pinnacle.

They reached the top, gasping for breath and calling out apologies to the middle-aged folks they'd shoved past. Valin was far below, rushing to catch them but still a few minutes away.

"Okay, now what?" Mack gasped.

"Yes, now what?" Dietmar echoed.

"Hey! I thought you knew!"

Dietmar looked very serious. "I have been here many times, it is true. After all, this place is on our family crest. But—"

"Your what now?"

"Our family crest. The coat of arms of the

Detmold branch of the von Augestein dynasty. The symbol of our family. It shows the helmet of Helmut der Zusammenhanglos—Helmut the Incoherent— the greatest of the von Augesteins in the fourteenth century, renowned for his inability to make anything clear. Below Helmut's helmet are three black lions above the Externsteine. And of course our family motto, which was written by Helmut and is therefore completely incoherent."

"The incoherent thing seems to have been passed on," Jarrah said. "Didn't understand a word of that. And by the way: ticktock! That crazy kid is coming!"

Xiao seemed mildly irritated by Jarrah. "You should not show disrespect for Dietmar's ancestors."

Mack said, "Why is the motto incoherent?"

Dietmar shrugged. "It is written in a strange alphabet, symbols that mean nothing."

Jarrah's curiosity beat out her skepticism. "Can you draw them here? The symbols, I mean."

"I have nothing to draw with."

Jarrah stuck her finger in her mouth and used the spit to draw on a flat altar.

"Ah," Dietmar said with obvious distaste. "Of

course I know the symbols. The family crest is on all our dinner plates; I have often puzzled over it."

He drew.

Valin raced.

Stefan blocked his path at one end of a short but scary bridge.

"It's Vargran!" Jarrah said, watching as Dietmar finished. "And it says . . ." Jarrah frowned, concentrating. "It says, 'Open the stairway to heaven.' I think. Of course, if you were speaking Vargran, you'd say, '*Sec-et eb etchi n(ch) alinea.*'"

Mack flinched. He looked around. He breathed a sigh of relief. "I was halfway expecting something crazy to happen."

Dietmar was obviously deeply impressed by what Jarrah had told him. "I cannot believe that after many centuries we know that our family motto is *Sec-et eb etchi n(ch) alinea.*"

Mack flinched again. And this time he was right to flinch because suddenly the ground began to shake.

"Earthquake!" Mack cried.

"We have no earthquakes in Germany!" Dietmar protested.

"You do now," Jarrah said. "Welcome to the Magnificent Twelve!"

"Hey, all you people, get off these rocks!" Mack yelled to the middle-aged tourists.

Dietmar yelled it in German. Roughly, *"Getten zee offen den rocks!"* At least that's how it sounded to Mack.

People were running, pelting back down the stairs and across the connecting bridges. People will do that in an earthquake: they will run and they will totally pelt. And as luck would have it, Valin was unprepared for the pelting. He was swept away by the frightened hordes.

The Externsteine was shaking. The rock pillars were swaying back and forth like tween girls at a Ke$ha concert. The gloomy little lake was rippled and splashing.

Unfortunately Mack didn't have the option of running. He just mostly had to stand there atop the pillar, hands out for balance, like a surfer trying to ride a really big wave.

Stefan made his way to his side and said a thoughtful, deeply impressed "Huh."

The smallest of the pillars suddenly upended with a great noise of ripping roots and flying dirt. It rolled end over end, like a slow baton, and snugged up against the next pillar.

These two pillars then crunched and ripped and tore and pushed themselves right up against Mack's pillar.

They formed now a sort of crude three-step staircase. A staircase you might climb if you had extremely long legs.

With a surge of dark green water, a new pillar began to rise from the lake. It pushed its way straight up, spilling water and mud and algae all down its side.

It rose higher, all the way up to where Mack and the others were standing.

"Come on!" Mack yelled.

He leaped onto the rising pillar. He landed hard, stumbled, took two way-too-big steps to try and steady himself, and almost launched off the edge.

But Stefan's hand grabbed him and yanked him back.

Still another pillar was growing now, even as the one they were on was still rising. The latest pillar was surging from the lake, catching up to them.

"It's a stairway!" Mack gasped.

They leaped, all together, onto the next pillar as it surged past them, impossibly big, and all covered with amazing carvings—lions, unicorns, weird things that none of them recognized, symbols, and figures of giant bearded dudes and women with severe braided hair.

Up they went. Mack leaned out to see if any more steps were coming, but this seemed like it.

"Look!" Xiao cried.

The pillar, the final stair, pushed up toward a door that hung all by itself in the air. A large door that led, as far as Mack could tell, to nothing at all.

Twenty-five

The door frame was a pointed arch of stone, all of it entwined with stone snakes and shields and spears and other not-very-welcoming things.

The door itself was made of trees. Not wood. Saying "wood" implies nice little two-by-fours or maybe a sheet of plywood. This door was built of logs as big as redwoods. They still had the bark on. And they were bound together with fat bands of iron bristling with barbed spikes.

The pillar came to a stop. It was still wet and a bit slimy with lake water. Mack and the others were probably five hundred feet in the air. High as a skyscraper. High enough not to hear the cameras clicking away below or the cries of amazement. But not so high that they couldn't see a lot of stunned, antlike tourists gaping. The inevitable phones and cameras were aimed up at them.

And there were Nine Iron and Valin. They were too far away for Mack to be sure of their expressions, but neither seemed to be raging or threatening. They seemed disturbingly calm.

"There's a sign on the door," Jarrah said.

Dietmar peered at it. "It says, 'Beware of Wolf.' In German and I think in Swedish and Danish, too."

"'Beware of wolf'?" Mack echoed. "There's a wolf?"

There was definitely a door knocker. It was a massive iron ball on a hinge. There was zero chance any of them could lift it.

"Should we knock?" Xiao asked.

"Like anyone would hear?" Jarrah said.

"Do we even want it to open?" Xiao wondered aloud.

Mack sighed. "Grimluk said we had to discover secret places. Get help from ancient ones. He sent us here, right?"

He knocked on the door. It made a very small sound.

"I think I know what is behind this door," Xiao said.

"I as well," Dietmar said.

Stefan kicked the door. Three times. As hard as he could without breaking his foot. That didn't make much noise, either, but it got a response.

A howl.

No, that doesn't quite express it. More like: HOW-OOOOOOOO-OOOWWLL!

Like that.

Mack, Jarrah, Xiao, and Dietmar jumped. If you added up all the jumps together, you'd have an Olympic record. Stefan did not jump. But he did say, "Huh."

The door opened with a sudden jerk. The motion of the door almost sucked them in.

Standing there holding the knob and scowling was a giant. He was probably fourteen feet tall. He had massive, bunched, oiled, tanned muscles. He had a blond beard almost down to his waist. His eyes were blue and crazy-intense.

In his free hand he held a short leash attached to a very big collar that went around the neck of a wolf the size of a medium-large elephant.

But the wolf was much scarier than an elephant.

The wolf was gray, aside from its black nose and black eyes and very white teeth. It, too, had crazy-intense eyes.

It made a sound approximately like "Grrrr-grr." Very low and deep in its throat.

All of this was alarming to Mack.

But despite the fact that Mack knew he should be focusing on the wolf's slavering jaws—jaws that could without the slightest doubt not just blow your house down, little pig, little pig, but chew it and swallow it no matter how many hairs you had on your chinny-chin-chin—Mack found his gaze drawn irresistibly to two very odd details.

First, the giant bearded guy was wearing sweat pants and a Led Zeppelin T-shirt. The pants were pale blue with a yellow stripe down the side. The T-shirt was stretched so tight over the massive upper body that it was like a grown man wearing a baby T. The giant's stomach was bare, revealing at least half of a six-pack.

The second thing, even more astounding, was that around the giant's neck hung what was unquestionably the biggest electric guitar in the world.

"What do you want?" the giant roared.

They stared, not quite knowing how to answer. Because none of them had a lot of experience dealing with giant wolf-wrangling guitar players.

Finally Mack said, "Um . . ."

"Well?"

"We're, um, we're the Magnificent Twelve. Or four of them, anyway."

The giant blinked his crazed blue eyes. He got a sort of crafty look and smirked a bit privately. Then, with patently false surprise, he said, "Wow. Is it that late? I thought it was still the twentieth century."

"No," Mack said. "We're, um, it's, um, you know, the twenty-first."

The giant nodded. "Well, come on in, then."

Mack and the others hesitated.

He thought he intercepted a sly look between wolf and giant.

The giant broke into a grin. "Don't worry about

old Fenrir here. He won't eat you. Just give him a little scratch behind the ears."

Fenrir made what might be a wolf smile. Or not.

Mack stepped across the threshold. He swallowed hard, bit his lip, scrunched his eyes, and gingerly patted the wolf's ruff.

"Come on, I want you to hear this," the giant said. "And give me your honest opinion. Don't be scared: I don't do the whole Mjolnir thing anymore."

They followed the giant and the wolf through the door, which slammed shut behind them.

The room was not at all what they would have expected based on the door. It was big—it would have to be. The walls were massive tree trunks with white plaster between them. There were ancient tapestries that showed ancient battle scenes in faded, muddy colors. But it looked as if many more tapestries had once hung on these walls. And Mack could clearly see an empty place that had once boasted a chandelier.

And the room had some more modern elements. For one thing, IKEA furniture.

It was normal IKEA furniture, but about a dozen tables had been shoved together to form one wide but low table, at which this massive creature could not possibly sit and eat.

Nevertheless there was food on the table: half a dozen two-liter bottles of some unknown soda and several ripped-apart packs of cookies. There was also a vase being used as an ashtray.

At one end of the chamber stood a low stage, and on that stage were massive amps. Inhumanly big. Metallica sized.

"What's a Mjolnir?" Mack whispered.

Dietmar had gone even paler than his normal pale. "Mjolnir? You don't know Mjolnir? It's the hammer of Thor."

Twenty-six

BACK TO A LONG TIME AGO . . .

Nine Iron wasn't sure just what he was expecting the Pale Queen to be like. Probably a queen. Like Queen Victoria, who had died and was widely admired by the English for having never had any fun, ever.

"So, tell me," Nine Iron said to Risky's back as they walked down yet another tunnel. "What's she like, your mother?" He was already thinking the Pale

Queen might someday be his mother-in-law.

Poor fool.

"Well, she's very friendly; she likes to crochet and arrange flowers, and loves long walks on the beach."

"Really?"

"No, you idiot. She's the Mother of All Monsters. And you're supposed to be an assassin? It's a good thing you're not interviewing for the mastermind position. Do you even realize that we're inside the Pale Queen?"

"Inside?"

"These tubes, they're all part of her. Through this series of tubes—what we call the intraweb—she gives birth to and then dispatches her minions. The tubes are connected to the world above and all through the World Beneath. Although the three-thousand-year curse has closed off just about all the world-above connections. Nowadays mostly she has to reach outside the frame."

Just to make conversation and to ward off his own nervousness, Nine Iron said, "What's that mean, outside the frame?"

Risky stopped. She turned back to him. They both stood still. "Maybe you're smarter than you look after all. But you'd pretty much have to be, wouldn't you?"

Nine Iron said, "Yes?"

"Say you have a picture, right? A photograph? A painting? You put it in a frame. You stare at that picture long enough, it's almost like you fall into that painting. That becomes the world you know: whatever is inside the frame. Stare long enough, and you can't even see what's outside the frame. But you know what, Paddy 'Nine Iron' Trout of County Grind?" She plucked at his collar and gave him a little slap.

Anyone else who ever did that to Nine Iron would have lived (briefly) to regret it. He wouldn't have let the biggest, scariest, most scarred-up, glowering, evil, squinting thug pluck his collar and slap his cheek. Because Nine Iron didn't fear guys like that.

But there was something about this redheaded young woman that told him he'd best just stand there and take whatever she dished out.

Paddy had never had anyone stand up to him the way Risky did. She wasn't afraid of him at all. He might as well have been a fly rather than a feared member of the Nafia.

He kind of liked the way she had slapped him.

At that moment her beauty, her fearlessness, and of course the sheer mind-boggling evil that seemed to emanate from her like some intoxicating perfume made him fall just a little in love with her.

Paddy knew at that moment that he would never marry any other woman. Where would he ever find a woman as completely pitiless, cold, and just plain rotten as Risky?

He knew as well that he could never tell her of his love. Because she would totally kill him.

Oh, absolutely.

In a heartbeat.

So he would have to bury his infatuation deep down inside.

Risky leaned close. "I'll tell you, Paddy: there's a great deal that exists outside of that frame. Come. I'll show you something."

He followed her. He would have followed her anywhere.

She moved faster now, as though she was moving with new purpose, excited, anticipating.

"Oh, I'll definitely show you something," she said, and laughed in her delightfully demonic-psychopathic-creepy way.

Suddenly the tunnel came to an end.

They stepped out onto a plateau, a sort of mesa, or maybe just a broad, wide platform. Beyond the plateau the ground fell away out of view. But it glowed down there; it glowed with a rainbow of colors that sent wild shadows up to the vaulted stone roof far, far overhead.

Nine Iron had a sense of a space so vast you could have put all of County Grind there and had space left over for all of New York.

He had expected something out of Dante. Not that he had read Dante. But in any case, he'd expected dark and gloom and maybe glowing red lava.

He had not expected this manic swirling of color. It was darkness, yes, but very colorful darkness. And yet, none of the colors cheered him up the way colors were supposed to.

When he looked closer, he began to see the reason for this. The colors came from millions of tiny whirls, like small tornadoes each united in a swath of millions of similar tornadoes of light, all forming one impossibly vast swirl.

They moved closer to the edge of the mesa, and Nine Iron found it very strange that he was sweating, because it wasn't that hot, really. And he found it strange that he was dragging his feet, because it wasn't like him to be afraid of something he couldn't see.

He certainly found it strange to feel his own heart, no longer an ignored source of rhythmic thumping, now like an animal struggling to pummel its way out of his chest.

"I don't . . . ," he said through lips now cracked, speaking with a tongue dry as dirt.

"Did you know that white light refracts into every other color?" Risky asked him.

"Um . . . My heart . . . it . . ."

In a singsong voice, Risky called out, "Mommy, Mom-meeee. I have a visitor."

"I don't . . ."

"Every soul casts its own light; did you know that, Paddy? Even the darkest of souls casts a light all its own."

A whimper was swallowed deep in Nine Iron's choked throat. How could he be so afraid and so in love? There had to be something wrong with him. (Well, duh.)

"Did you think she was the Pale Queen because she didn't get enough sun, Paddy? No, no, no. She is the Pale Queen because she is made up of so many lost souls, all swirling together in their many hues to create one brilliant light."

Nine Iron wanted to say something along the lines of "That's great to know, thanks for the lesson, I'm outta here." But he was in no condition to say anything at all because his heart was like the heart of a whale, filling his whole inside with an intolerable pounding.

"She can take any shape, my mother, any shape or form. A conquering worm, a spider as big as a ship, a creature of blades and spikes. But you, Nine Iron, you will see her as she is."

He could no longer force his feet forward. So Risky, laughing gaily, grabbed his arm and hauled him mercilessly to the edge. Dread and infatuation were at war in Paddy's poor, confused brain.

"Now gaze upon the Pale Queen," Risky crowed.

Nine Iron did.

And he fell to his knees.

And from that moment forward there was absolutely zero chance that Paddy "Nine Iron" Trout would ever serve anyone but the Mother of All Monsters, or love anyone but Ereskigal.

Twenty-seven

I t took Mack a few seconds to put what Dietmar had just said together in his head. "Wait, are you telling me that's Thor?"

As if in answer, the bearded giant hopped up onto the stage and plugged his guitar into the amp.

"Okay, I'm not trying to say I'm Jimmy Page or Hendrix or anything, but I think I just about have this down."

He waved a hand behind him, an almost careless gesture. And suddenly there was a flash of lightning and a peal of thunder.

A decidedly non-god-sized human appeared, perched on a stool behind the drum kit. He had a brown beard and long hair.

But the first sound was from Thor's guitar. An urgent, insistent riff that built in intensity.

A bass player appeared, just popped into view. Added his urgency to Thor's.

And then the drummer started in.

They rocked for about thirty seconds until Thor yelled, "No, no, no! That's not it. Why can't I get it right?" He held out his guitar and glared at it like it just wasn't doing what he wanted it to do.

The music stopped. The drummer shrugged.

Thor looked embarrassed. "Work in progress," he said to Mack and the others. "Work in progress. But wait. I have one for you; it's, like, my theme song." He looked over his shoulder at the drummer. "'Immigrant Song.' One, two, three, four . . ."

The drummer started beating out a tattoo.

Thor played a rhythmic riff.

And out of nowhere three very intimidating-looking women with long blond braids appeared and began singing in high-pitched wails, "Ah ah ah aaah! Ah ah ah aaah!"

Thor sang:

*"We come from the land of the ice and snow,
From the midnight sun where the hot springs blow...."*

He was just launching into a second verse of "Immigrant Song" when a far door crashed open and an old guy, about a foot taller than Thor, stomped in.

"I'm trying to watch the match!"

This second god—because that's clearly what he was—looked like an older, meaner Thor. But without the ludicrous T-shirt. This god was dressed the part, with a gold shield over his chest, gold bands around his bare arms, tall boots, and a sword clanking at his side.

But the outfit looked less than impressive. The hem of his tunic was frayed; the gold was smudged and seemed to be marked with some dried food.

"I'm just trying to entertain our guests!" Thor protested. But he waved his hand and disappeared the rest of the band. "You know," he said significantly. "Our guests?"

"Oh, yes. Of course," the ancient muttered. "Good, good. It's about time. We're completely out of Gouda."

"Kids," Thor said, "this is Odin. Or Wotan if you're speaking German. Odin, these are . . ." Thor hesitated. "Should I intro you as the Magnificent Twelve or what?"

Mack said, "That would be great. Sir." He thought about that for a beat; *sir* didn't seem like quite enough. So he added, "Your Highness."

"Welcome," Thor said with a grand sweep of his hand, "to Asgard!" Then, as if realizing how it must look to strangers, he added, "You should have seen it back in the day."

There was a rustle of fabric dragging on stone. Mack saw a third person, quite unlike either Thor or Odin. More human-scale, though still rather tall. She was very dark skinned, with black-in-black eyes and jet-black hair that reached all the way to the floor.

Looking closer, Mack saw many tiny stars glittering in the depths of those eyes. Her formfitting dress was actually in a lunar pattern, like a blown-up photograph of the gray and white surface of the moon.

Mack looked at her and yawned. So did Jarrah, Dietmar, and Stefan.

"Nott, goddess of the night," Thor explained unnecessarily.

Nott spoke in a dreamy, faraway voice. "Welcome." Then, since they were all having a hard time keeping their eyes open, she added, "Oh, good grief, I'd forgotten how vulnerable mortals are." She snapped her fingers. "Stay awake."

Mack's cell phone signaled a message. Mack, Odin, Thor, and Nott all reached for their phones at the same time.

"Huh," Stefan commented.

"You guys get service here?" Mack asked, incredulous. "Aren't we, like, in magic land or something?"

Nott explained. "We are not confined; it is you who are limited. Humans see the world as if peering through a straw. They choose not to see us."

"Exactly," Thor boomed. "Doesn't mean we can't have BlackBerries. I mean, my manager has to be able to get hold of me. He could have a gig for me."

"You play gigs?" Jarrah asked skeptically.

"All over Germany, Denmark, up in Sweden,

Norway. Not stadiums, that's not my thing. I mean, it's mostly small clubs. But I like the intimacy, the audience feedback. You know?" He stroked his blond beard. "I haven't played a lot of gigs lately. . . . I guess it's been a while." He sighed and seemed a little sad.

Then Thor clapped his hands together and said, "Hey! You guys thirsty? Flagon of ale?"

Mack left it to Jarrah to decline the offer of a beer.

Xiao gave Mack a significant look and began a whispered conversation with Nott.

Mack checked his message:

> Don't worry, Mack; Mom says she will replace laptop since I need it for school. Next time: no chisels!

Mack sighed deeply. He'd loved that laptop. All his files would probably be lost. All his games. None of which, he realized with a secret smile, were nearly as cool as hanging out with the gods of Asgard. Even this decrepit Asgard.

Xiao left Nott's side and came back to Mack. Smiling all the while, Xiao whispered, "We are being deceived."

Before he could ask what she was talking about, Thor launched into an earsplitting solo. So what Xiao said next had to be shouted into his ear.

"NOTT SAYS IT'S ALL A TRAP!"

"WHAT?"

"THEY'RE GIVING US TO THE PALE QUEEN!"

Odin had left, muttering something about the music. Thor whaled on his guitar. Nott carefully avoided meeting anyone's eye.

"WHY?"

"I DON'T KNOW!"

You know how sometimes you'll be at a party and the music is really loud, so you have to shout to be heard? And then suddenly the music stops, and you're still shouting?

Thor's guitar solo ended abruptly on the word "I."

Which left Xiao yelling, "DON'T KNOW."

The giant blond god took off his guitar and laid it aside. "What is it you don't know?" Thor demanded, with a sidelong glance at Nott.

"So many things," Mack said. "Such as . . . well . . . such as, where's the bathroom?"

Cold blue suspicion filled Thor's eyes. He shot a distrustful look at Nott. "We're not that formal around here. There's a jar over there."

Mack saw a flower vase he recognized from his own living room. Definitely IKEA.

"No. It's number two," Mack said.

"Ah."

"In fact, we all have to go number two."

Jarrah, Dietmar, and Stefan stared at Mack.

Fenrir sauntered toward them. His wolf breath reached them first.

"That's right," Mack blustered. "We all need a bathroom." He tried out a weak smile. "It's all the travel. You know."

"I'll show them where to go," Nott volunteered.

There followed a very long pause during which Thor looked nervously toward the doorway through which Odin had disappeared. He licked his giant lips uncertainly. Then he shrugged.

"If you gotta go, you gotta go."

"Right this way," Nott said.

"Don't be long," Thor said, with no trace of the openhearted bonhomie he'd shown thus far. "Fenrir will miss you."

Twenty-eight

Nott led them along a hallway you could have taxied a 747 down. Here, too, there were blank spaces where tapestries had once hung, and spots where darker flooring suggested there had once been furniture.

Part of Mack was actually relieved. He finally knew where the trap was. Grimluk must have suspected the Pale Queen would try to reach out to Odin and his brood.

The bathroom was interesting. Mack wasn't quite sure what he had expected. But he had not expected a gray granite counter with two giant oval holes.

This counter was god-height, appropriate for a fourteen-foot-tall person, not so useful for people under six feet.

Mack stood on his toes to see that the holes did not lead to a bowl, or even a pipe. Or a hole in the ground.

"Those are clouds," Jarrah said. "Well, that's pretty high and mighty."

The oval holes opened directly onto the tops of fluffy white clouds.

"It's over the sea," Nott said a little defensively.

"Bad luck for some poor fisherman, eh?" Jarrah huffed. "A little present from the gods?"

Xiao was the only one who seemed really upset. "This is very wrong behavior," she said to Nott. "With great power comes great responsibility."

Nott curled her lip. "Is that your precious Confucius?"

"Spider-Man's dad," Stefan said.

"That's his uncle, not his dad," Jarrah said. "Uncle Ben."

"Huh."

"I believe Socrates said something like it, too," Xiao said. "I was translating loosely."

"Naw, it was Uncle Ben," Jarrah insisted.

"The point," Xiao said, gritting her teeth, "is that just because you are a god or a dragon or any other powerful being, you don't have a right to literally—"

"Enough," Nott interrupted. "I'm only tolerating you out of affection for Shen Long. And because I have the knowledge you need to defeat the Mother of All Monsters. But I won't be lectured by a mortal. Or a dragon, for that matter."

"And we are grateful for you helping us," Mack interrupted smoothly. "But what do you mean, help us defeat the Pale Queen?"

"Why do you think Grimluk sent you to the Externsteine?" Nott asked.

"To find me, of course," Dietmar said.

"Perhaps, in part," Nott said. "But also so that I may give you this." She held out a small stone disk, no bigger than a DVD, but quite a bit heavier. It was covered, edge to edge, with incredibly ornate scrollwork.

Mack took it. "Thanks," he said, looking at it

carefully. "What is it?"

"It is a key. The ancient key of the MacGuffins. You must take it to the tomb of William Blisterthöng MacGuffin. You will find the disk into which this one fits."

"Say what now? Tomb?" Mack said.

"He has been dead for a thousand years. Even in Scotland they don't just leave corpses lying out on park benches."

"And why exactly am I digging up a dead guy?"

"Because when this disk is centered in the outer disk, you will have many of the great Vargran words of power. The Vargran you must have to defeat the Pale Queen!"

"I'm sorry, I didn't track on anything after the part about digging up a dead guy," Mack said.

"I got it," Dietmar said.

"Yeah, well, so did I," Jarrah snapped.

"I, too, got it," Xiao said.

"Huh?" Stefan said.

"Here's what I get: probably we shouldn't all stay in the bathroom for much longer," Mack said. "Thor will get suspicious."

"Thor is an idiot," Nott said. "But Fenrir will come

to investigate. We must hurry. If we can reach the observatory, you may escape with your lives. The observatory is where All-Father Odin watches what happens in the world of humans. Mostly sports. Football, and the Olympics. It is why we keep the back door to the Externsteine in existence: Odin is a big supporter of Arminia Bielefeld and likes to attend actual matches in disguise."

In response to Mack's quizzical look, Dietmar said, "It is the local football team. Soccer to you."

"Why would Thor sell us out? He seemed like a nice guy," Mack protested.

That actually brought a laugh from Nott. And she didn't strike any of them as a giggly person.

"Thor? A nice guy?" Nott said. "And no doubt Odin seemed like a weary old man. But listen, young fool: in the olden days of yore, the Vikings used to raid in their longships. They would arrive at first light, taking a small town by surprise and catching people in their beds. They would seem like demons to the townsfolk. Every atrocity you can possibly imagine would take place. And always the cries of 'Wotan' and 'Thor' were on the lips of the berserkers."

"Berserkers?" Stefan asked. He liked the sound of that.

"The berserker state," Nott said distastefully. "It is a madness that seizes warriors, a madness sent by All-Father Odin. A madness so wild, so fierce, so fearless, so enraged that no foe could stand against them, and even their friends kept away lest they be slaughtered in the heat of it."

"Huh," Stefan said. "Cool."

"But why would he sell us out?" Mack demanded.

"Have you not noticed the shabbiness and decay that is Asgard?" Nott asked. "We are forgotten by those who once worshipped us. Our economy is in shambles. Once men sacrificed to us: food, weapons, gold. Now we are reduced to selling the tapestries and furnishings at the Gammel Strand flea market in Copenhagen."

"So you're getting paid to give us up?" Jarrah asked.

"The Pale Queen is very rich," Nott explained. "She never relied on sacrifices for income. Instead she pillaged and then invested wisely. She invested in cell phone carriers, airlines, and health insurers—anything evil. And of course she owns several banks. Whereas we . . . well, All-Father Odin was never a wise steward. So our gold was spent on beer and sausages, and our antiques were sold. All we have left now is our minority share of Lego." Nott sighed. "We're reduced to shopping the sales at the Aldi."

"A discount chain," Dietmar explained.

"Ah. Like Costco." Mack nodded.

Mack opened the door a crack and peeked out into the hallway. "I think it's clear."

"Then let us go," Nott said.

"So long as it's not on anyone's head," Xiao said.

Stefan laughed and offered her a high five, which Xiao stared at blankly.

Nott led the way out of the bathroom. She glided. The rest of them trotted as quietly as they could.

Mack saw a blue-green glow ahead. The observatory. Although what exactly that meant was a mystery to him.

"I guess it was cooler for you gods in the old days," Mack said in a low voice, searching for something polite to say to smooth over the argument between Xiao and Nott.

"Yes," the booming voice of Thor said. "It was

cooler in the old days."

He stepped into view, filling the arch at the far end of the hall. He still had his guitar, but the T-shirt and sweatpants were gone. Now he wore tall leather boots, sketchy deerskin leggings, a threadbare orange-red knee-length tunic, and what looked like the mangy skin of one very large bear over his shoulders.

He did not have a helmet, let alone one with horns.

He did, however, have a very impressive belt hung with a very wicked-looking sword.

Nott said, "Let them go, Thor. The old days are dead and gone. You cannot bring them back, not even with the Pale Queen's money."

Thor's cold blue eyes stared at her with open contempt. "Three thousand years ago the Pale Queen was taken and bound. And for a long while after, we still kept our power, Nott. But each year it faded. Just a little at first. But little by little . . . And now look at me. Gaze with pity and contempt upon he who was once the god of thunder!"

"Dude," Mack said. "No one was dissing you. You are still totally Thor."

"Very much so," Jarrah said. "Excellently Thorlike."

But Dietmar said, "We have no need of such silly things as gods of thunder."

"Sure we do," Mack said, trying to catch Dietmar's eye and get him to play along. "I think everyone should have a god of thunder."

But Dietmar wasn't having it. He stood with hands on hips, defiant. "You should be ashamed of your behavior, you so-called god of thunder, threatening us this way."

"No, no," Mack said tersely. "He's totally cool with the whole giant boots and sword thing and all."

"No. He is just a big bully," Dietmar insisted.

"Emphasis on big," Jarrah said. "So maybe we should all be a bit more polite, eh, mate?"

"Nonsense. He can squash us like insects, but that is no reason for us to flatter him."

"Actually—" Mack started to say.

But he stopped when he felt very large, very meat-scented breath coming from behind him. He turned slowly, and there stood Fenrir, grinning his wolf grin.

"Gentle, Fenrir, gentle," Thor said. "Hel will want them alive. You know she likes her meat fresh."

Mack was busy calculating the distance to the

green-blue glow of the observatory beyond Thor. It was only a hundred yards or so. A hundred yards and one giant thunder god.

Plus one very giant wolf.

"You're trying to reach the observatory?" Thor said, smirking. "Well, go ahead. I'm not as quick as I used to be when I worked out in battle every day. Run for it."

Mack had no particular phobia involving giant gods. And he'd had quite a bit of experience dealing with bullies. But this wasn't like the old days of trying to outthink or outrun Stefan.

"Any of you guys have anything?" Mack whispered.

Xiao said, "Vargran spells will not work on gods. Except indirectly. If you had a spell to turn yourself into one of them, and a spell to give yourself a big magical spear . . ." Xiao blushed. "I realize that's not very helpful."

"We must not let them push us around," Dietmar added stoutly.

"That's even less helpful," Mack said.

He took a deep breath. He had an idea. But it wasn't a very good one. He turned to face Fenrir. The wolf was as big as an elephant.

"Hey, Fenrir, are you one of those wolves who like to dress up in women's clothing and try to pass as Grandma?" Mack asked the world's largest wolf.

Fenrir's yellow eyes narrowed to slits.

"I mean, it's amazing, really, how lame wolves are," Mack went on. "Outsmarted by Little Red Riding Hood. Killed and cooked by the Three Little Pigs."

"Lies," Thor said. "Myths."

"Dude, you're a myth," Mack said, turning back to him. "I mean, what a disappointment. You're supposed to be all crazy-tough and dangerous, and instead you're some pitiful Guitar Hero wanna-be."

Then, back to Fenrir. "And what's even more pathetic is your big dog."

A growl pitched somewhere around the sound a jet engine makes when it sucks in a goose escaped from Fenrir.

"Don't call him a dog!" Thor cried. The concern in his voice was genuine; Mack was sure of it. He was already putting his hands out in a calming gesture.

Yes, that was it: the pressure point, the thing he could do to really infuriate the wolf.

"Can you do any tricks, Fenrir? Can you roll over? Can you shake hands? Can you play dead?" In a low murmur to his friends, he said, "When he jumps, go through Thor's legs."

The growl deepened, the ruff of fur on Fenrir's shoulders stood up, and he seemed to swell in size. But still Fenrir did not attack.

"My friend has a dog just like you," Mack said. "And you know what? He eats his own poop."

Fenrir's leap was so sudden and so powerful, Mack was almost caught standing.

It was stunning to see something so large move with such shocking speed.

Mack bolted. Jarrah, Xiao, and Dietmar reacted with speed that almost equaled Mack's. But frankly, no one could beat Mack when it came to bully dodging. And Stefan had no experience at all with running away.

So what happened was this: Mack leaped for the gap between Thor's tree-trunk legs. He cleared the obstacle and was flying down the polished stone hallway at about the speed of sound when he realized that Xiao, Jarrah, and Dietmar had collided trying to squeeze through.

And Stefan was still standing around. He was just not any good at terrified fleeing.

And Fenrir was flying through the air.

So Mack yelled, "Look out!"

Stefan crouched beneath Fenrir's hairy belly; the wolf flew over him and slammed into his master, who was yelling in a scared god voice, "Fenrir, down! Down, boy!"

The wolf, the god, the three kids—well, two kids and one dragon passing as a kid—wrapped themselves into one big bowling ball of deerskin, fur, sword, and tangled limbs.

Jarrah was quickest to recover. She yanked Dietmar to his feet and hauled butt toward Mack. Stefan jumped atop Fenrir, bounced off his back, avoided a wild grab by a prostrate Thor, and landed—grinning hugely—on the safe side of the gaggle.

Only Xiao was still trapped. She was sort of squashed beneath one of Fenrir's shoulders.

Mack's every instinct told him to keep running. But in that terrifying moment he came to realize a really dreadful truth: it was the Magnificent Twelve.

Not the Magnificent Eleven. Or Ten. Or any smaller number.

They were like the Three Musketeers, except there would be Twelve Musketeers. So instead of all-for-one-and-one-for-all times three, it was going to be all-for-one-and-one-for-all times twelve—which meant not losing anyone. Not Xiao, not Jarrah, not Dietmar. Not even that traitor Valin. And managing all that was going to be really difficult.

One other thing he realized. He was one of the Twelve and he, too, was not expendable. Stefan, on the other hand . . .

"Stefan! Get Xiao!" Mack yelled.

Stefan spun like an athlete and ran straight back at the god-wolf tangle.

Stefan didn't grab Xiao's up-stretched hand. Instead he grabbed the hilt of Thor's sword.

He pulled. And pulled. Straining his muscles.

Thor was fourteen feet tall. His sword was a good six feet—longer than Stefan was tall—and it was not made of some lightweight space-age polymer. This was old-fashioned steel and gold and bronze and other heavy things.

Stefan was strong. But he was not god-strong. He could draw the sword but, beyond that, all he could do was drag it across the floor.

"Huh," Stefan remarked.

Fortunately Jarrah had something more intelligent to say. She said, "*Esk-ma belast!*"

And Stefan began to grow.

Twenty-nine

Stefan began to grow. But it didn't happen very fast. What did happen fast was Fenrir and Thor untangling from each other. Xiao slipped out from under them unnoticed. Stefan pulling on Thor's sword had definitely stolen the spotlight.

Now Stefan was sort of dragging the sword across the floor. The point left a scratch.

Thor threw back his head and laughed. "Will you swing Thor's sword? I don't think so, little boy."

Stefan was just getting close to six feet. So he was almost as tall as the sword now. But he was still a long way from going all ninja with it.

Thor wrapped his massive fist around Stefan's throat.

"Wait!" Mack yelled. "Wait! I thought you enjoyed battle. I thought that was the Asgard way."

Thor looked at Stefan, now dangling with his feet off the floor and the sword still dragging. "Battle? With this child?"

Thor laughed again, and this time Fenrir joined in. One doesn't normally think of wolves laughing. And one would be right about that. What Fenrir did was a sort of huffing, snorting sound that could have been laughter but could also have been asthma.

"Look! He's growing!" Mack said. "If you don't kill him, he'll be big enough to take you on."

Thor looked at Stefan. He weighed him in his hand and nodded thoughtfully. Stefan was definitely growing. As if to prove the point, Stefan lifted the sword up off the floor and made a feeble pendulum swing with it.

"Battle," Thor said, relishing the word like a toddler

with the word *candy*, or a parent with the word *sleep*.

Nott spoke up. "Would the thunder god show himself to be a coward in front of Hel?"

"Is she here?" Thor asked nervously.

"Not yet," Nott said. "But just as Fenrir is not your dog, you are not hers. Or are you?"

"Do not provoke me," Thor hissed. He set Stefan down. Actually Stefan had almost set himself down by virtue of continuing to grow. He was NBA sized now. And unlike the Lepercons, Stefan's muscles seemed to grow in proportion.

Stefan took a couple of staggering steps back, and now he managed to actually level the sword, point aimed at Thor's heart.

Thor smiled. "But I have no weapon," Thor said. "Just my guitar."

As Mack and the others stared helplessly, Thor's massive guitar began to change shape. The strings smoked and evaporated. The neck shortened and thickened. The body lost its bright-polished sheen and became dull gray stone. Plus it looked a lot more like a two-headed ax.

"Every guitar should have a name," Thor said. "Do

you know what my guitar is called?"

Mack shook his head.

But Dietmar nodded yes; he'd guessed. "Mjolnir," Dietmar whispered.

"MJOLNIR!" Thor roared.

He grabbed the stone ax by its short handle and laughed like the crazy Viking god-warrior he was. "Mjolnir! The hammer of THOOOOOR!"

To emphasize his point, he held it over his head. Lightning shot from it in a dozen bolts, sizzling the remaining hanging tapestries and singeing Fenrir's fur.

"Flee, human! Flee from the wrath of mighty Thor!"

To which Stefan said, "No."

Stefan—now only a few feet shorter than Thor, and very able to lift the sword—ran straight at Thor with the sword pointed like a lance.

Stone hit steel, and Thor batted the sword away with practiced ease. Thor hadn't become thunder god by not knowing how to fight.

But Stefan hadn't become King of All Bullies by being a wuss.

Stefan took the momentum and swung a 360, came

around with his blade low and horizontal, aiming at Thor's legs. The sword bit. It sliced into Thor's leggings. But stopped there.

Stefan drew the sword back. There was blood on the blade.

For what felt like way too long a pause, Thor stared at the blood. So did Fenrir. And everyone else, too.

Thor began to breathe hard. His face grew red. His eyes bulged. The veins and tendons on his thick neck all stood out. His grip on the hammer tightened so much you could hear something snapping—probably his sinews, but maybe the actual granite.

"Berserker!" Nott cried. "Run! Run away! He is going berserk!"

Thor took Mjolnir, screamed something incoherent, and threw it with all his might straight at Stefan. Stefan fortunately was not one of those big muscle-bound guys who are slow and clumsy. Stefan was quick as a snake. He bent back, and the massive hammer went flying past his chest—so close that it ripped his shirt.

Mack was almost knocked over by the wind of the hammer's passing. The tapestries flapped like laundry on a line in a gale. Nott's gown whipped. Fenrir's fur ruffled.

Mjolnir flew all the way down the hall. It smashed into the distant wall—*crash!*—with a sound like a freeway pileup. And then, impossibly, it came flying straight back to Thor's high-held hand.

"Huh," Stefan remarked. "Excellent."

Stefan grabbed the front of his lacerated shirt, yanked it off, and tossed it aside. He was about twelve feet tall now, a giant with glistening muscles.

"Oh yeah, that'll do," Jarrah said admiringly. Then added, "I meant he's big enough now to fight."

"Muscles are not so important," Dietmar muttered through pursed lips.

Thor wasn't waiting around for Stefan to get any bigger. With a bellow that literally shook the walls, he leaped at Stefan.

Stefan slashed. Thor swung. Both missed.

They whirled past each other, came back around face-to-face, and Stefan raised the sword high and brought it down hard. It missed Thor's skull but hacked off a few inches of hair. The blow threw Thor off balance so he couldn't wield his hammer, but even falling away, he could kick. His boot caught Stefan in the chest and knocked him flying.

"Stefan!" Jarrah cried.

Stefan skidded halfway down the hallway on his back. His bare back skin made a squeegee sound.

"AAAAAAAAH!" Thor cried in loud triumph.

It had to be said that both Thor and Stefan seemed to be having a very good time.

But when Stefan got up, he had grown another several feet. He banged his head against the high, arched ceiling. He frowned, reached to one of the chandeliers, and pulled out what looked like a dark blue cloth.

"Someone want this?"

"My scarf!" Nott said. "So that's where it was."

Stefan had to squeeze to get his head around the chandelier and get back into the fight.

"He's getting too big," Mack said.

"I know. What's the Vargran for 'Stop growing'?"

"Like I know?" He felt Nott's disk in his pocket. The disk that supposedly could be combined with another to unlock Vargran power words. Why a stone disk? Did none of these people understand the concept of a computer file?

"I don't know 'stop.' I only know 'larger' and 'smaller.'"

Thor charged with a roar.

Stefan handled the sword like a toy now. He whipped it around in a circle of steel, like a lawn-mower blade.

Thor stopped charging. He drew back mighty Mjolnir, and there was no way he could possibly miss now. Not with Stefan basically filling the entire hall-way.

"*Esk-ma pateet!*" Jarrah yelled.

Mjolnir flew.

A bright turquoise-and-gold serpentine creature smacked into the hammer in midair. Mjolnir went flying harmlessly past Stefan, but knocked Xiao into a wall with a sickening crunch.

"Hey!" Stefan yelled. "I promised to get her back safe!"

He charged Thor—who was still waiting on Mjolnir to return—and stabbed him with the sword.

The sword went into Thor's side and opened him up like a gutted trout. . . . Well, it would have gone straight into Thor's side and opened him up like a gutted trout except that Stefan was shrinking. And he was shrinking even faster than he had grown. So instead of the trout-gutting move, it was a thigh-stabbing move.

Blood sprayed. It sprayed like a fire hose because there's no such thing as a berserker without high blood pressure.

"AAAARRGH!" Thor cried.

"Yeah, try that on," Stefan said. But it was less than effective as a triumphant gloat because he was getting a bit of a chipmunk sound in his voice as he shriveled like cashmere in a hot dryer.

Thor was yelling and dancing around in pain, holding the wound in his thigh. It was a good thing he was distracted, because Stefan was now just about hobbit sized, and that whole scene where the hobbit stabs the king of the Nazgûl in the foot is fine in a book or a movie, but this was real life.

"Make him grow again!" Mack cried.

"You can't repeat a spell in less than twenty-four hours!"

"Huh," Stefan said in an adorable little voice.

"Plan B: *ruuuun!*" Mack cried.

Xiao had recovered. She swooped low, snatched tiny Stefan up, and they all pelted past Thor, who was really being kind of a big baby about the wound in his thigh.

Mack, Jarrah, and Dietmar raced after her. Nott swept in behind them, providing a sort of shield from whatever Thor might throw their way next.

The observatory was just ahead. What exactly that meant for Mack, he wasn't sure.

Thirty

NOT VERY LONG AGO . . .

Paddy "Nine Iron" Trout grew old in the service of the Nafia and the Pale Queen. The world changed around him, going from bad to worse. Then back to bad. Then worse again.

He lived through wars and plagues and many terrible hard times. He survived them all. He even survived the departure of Simon Cowell from *American Idol*.

After long, long lives, his parents died.

First his father, who drank himself to death. No, not whiskey: sow's milk. It was the sow's milk of August. Never drink sow's milk in August. Sh! You don't need to know why: just don't.

Then, at the age of 121, Paddy's mother died of a broken hearth.

As you know, a hearth is a fireplace. And in County Grind all the cooking was done in the hearth. Mother Trout was getting quite old, and a little forgetful. She had prepared oat-stuffed bladder a thousand times before. But this time—who knows what may have distracted the poor dear—she forgot to pierce the bladder. In the heat of the hearth the bladder swelled, swelled, bigger and bigger, and with no way for the oat vapor to be released, it exploded. The hearth blew apart, killing Mother Trout instantly.

Paddy came to her funeral.

Well, actually he was on the way to kill a guy over in County Toyle and he thought, You know, while I'm here, I could finally kill Liam. That would have been a twofer.

But when he arrived at the old house, he saw

the terrible damage done, and in his heart he knew he couldn't kill Liam. Because with the house all destroyed, the farm was worthless. The last thing Paddy wanted to do was inherit a worthless farm. Far better to let Liam live out his miserable, impoverished days on a run-down oat farm.

So, actually, it was just coincidence that Paddy happened to arrive on the day of Mother Trout's funeral.

It was a solemn affair with all due ceremony.

Afterward Liam came over to Paddy and said, "So, what have you been up to this last nearly-a-century, little brother?"

"I've been working to enslave the human race and ensure the triumph of evil," Paddy said.

"Ah, so you're a mortgage broker. Did you never marry?"

"None of your concern, you dull-witted oat farmer," Paddy snapped.

But as he turned and walked away from County Grind, never to return, he remembered when he first met Ereskigal and had his heart broken as thoroughly as Mother Trout's hearth.

Paddy knew he would never know happiness. And

over the years he had begun to wonder if he would even live long enough to see the rise of the Pale Queen—the monster who could have been his mother-in-law if only things had worked out differently.

It was then, at a low point in Paddy's life, with old age and disappointment crowding around him, with his health failing, with his almost entirely green wardrobe no longer in fashion, that she, the princess Ereskigal, appeared to him again—unchanged by the years, except for her hairstyle—and told him that he had one last great task to perform.

"There is a second Twelve, Paddy," Risky said.

"Twenty-four?" he guessed.

"No, you doddering, gasping, wrinkled old fool, a new Magnifica, a second Twelve of Twelves. They mean to stop us."

Paddy's rheumy eyes glittered. His clotted lungs wheezed. "Has the first of the Twelve been revealed?"

Risky smiled her alluring yet not exactly warm smile and said, "His name is Mack."

She slipped her business card into his hand. It read, "Ereskigal. Evil Princess." And her email. But in pen she had written Mack's address and a description that was heavy on the use of the word *medium*.

"Kill him," Risky said. And for just a fleeting second as he took the card, his aged, arthritic, papery-skinned old fingers touched her hand and sent a shudder of disgust through her. "Kill him for Mom and me, Paddy."

With more energy and purpose than he had known in many, many (many) years, Paddy "Nine Iron" Trout turned on his heel and marched sloooowly away to kill once more for his only love.

Thirty-one

The observatory turned out to be a god's version of the ultimate TV room. It was a very large, spherical space made more cozy by massive timbers that held up the arched roof. Various stuffed heads had been mounted on the rough-hewn timbers: deer, elk, antelope, reindeer, wolf, wild boar, something that looked like a yak, something else that looked like a buffalo, something that may have been a dragon, and several somethings that definitely looked like humans.

Here, too, there were some empty spaces, where the best-looking heads had presumably been taken to the flea market.

All the remaining mounted heads had the fiercest expressions they could muster. It couldn't have been easy for the taxidermist to make a moose look murderous. Much easier with the human heads, who all seemed to have huge, bristly beards and crazy blue eyes.

But all that was just decoration—sort of the berserker version of a Zac Efron poster hanging on the wall. The interesting thing about the room was that there were twelve recessed circles on the stone floor, each containing water that went right up to the rim and threatened to spill out.

Above each round pool was a 3-D image: a soccer game, a meadow, a bear sleeping in a cave, a movie theater showing *Fantastic Mr. Fox 2: Chicken Apocalypse*, a circle of moldering old stones, a golden temple in the middle of a lake, another soccer match, what looked like an isolated house at night, and the caldera of a volcano.

One of the circles was out of order and the picture

was flickering in and out, more snow and static than picture.

It was the volcano that drew every eye. Because there, standing on a rocky promontory, was the princess Ereskigal. Or Hel as she was known around here.

Risky.

Mack had the unsettling feeling that Risky could see through the hologram and right into the observatory.

Odin, or Wotan, sat in a high throne. It looked pretty comfortable, piled deep with furs and plaid blankets. It was mounted on a sort of crude track that extended all the way around the room. By his hand Odin had a lever, like the ones you might see on a San Francisco cable car.

He was watching one of the soccer matches with great interest, leaning forward in his throne. But then he yanked the lever and his throne went scooting along its track, bringing him to a stop in front of the second soccer game.

Clearly TiVo had not made it to Asgard. And the channel-surfing method was primitive. On the other hand, this was some very real-looking 3-D.

"How do we escape?" Mack asked Nott.

She waved her hand to encompass the various holograms. "Each is a portal."

Xiao set Stefan down. He stood about two feet tall. She switched to her human look.

Risky coming from one direction. Thor—recovered from his wound but not recovered from the humiliation—and Fenrir from the other.

Time for a quick decision.

"Follow me!" Mack yelled. And he dived headfirst into the nearest pool. It happened to be one of the two soccer games.

If there was regular water in the pool, it sure didn't feel like it. In fact, it felt as if he was diving through a giant bubble. Not like it popped but like it kind of slid over his skin like a superthin membrane.

And all at once, there he was at midfield in the middle of a soccer game. Mack, Xiao, Jarrah, Dietmar, and a midget Stefan, all on the trampled grass.

Now, when you hear the words *soccer game*, maybe you're thinking about the kind of games you know from Saturday junior leagues all over the country, with girls or boys in bright uniforms sort of indifferently chasing a ball around while coaches yell unheeded advice and parents sit on the sidelines in fold-out chairs secretly checking their BlackBerries.

This wasn't like that.

In this game the players looked like they'd been constructed out of action figures. And where the parents would normally be sitting, there were something like thirty thousand people in a huge arc of stands.

At the exact instant Mack and his friends appeared, one of the players was taking a shot on goal. All thirty thousand people were on their feet shouting. Also gesticulating and making faces. (It's almost impossible to shout without also making faces, and once you've gone that far, you might as well gesticulate.)

In any case, it was a roar of noise.

Then the player noticed that there were four kids and a little person standing in the middle of the field. His foot missed. The ball flew wide.

The stadium went from frenzied roar to utter silence—silence so profound that Mack could hear his own heartbeat.

Thirty thousand pairs of eyes, totaling 59,999 eyes in all—an old dude up in row 14 had a glass eye, which doesn't really count—went from staring at the kicker and the goalkeeper to staring at the sudden apparition in midfield.

You could almost hear the eyeballs snap.

TV cameras swung around.

The camera that hung above the field on a wire scooted toward them.

"They've spotted us," Dietmar said.

"I believe you may be right," Mack said.

The crowd had indeed spotted them. And the crowd was not happy about it. Thirty thousand voices bellowed in outrage. Not astonishment or surprise or disbelief, mind you: outrage. Fury. Hatred. Because while it was definitely unusual for a bunch of kids to suddenly pop up in midfield, the really important thing was that the goal had been missed.

Black-and-white-striped officials ran at them.

Players from both teams ran at them, and they were faster and scarier.

And just as they were closing in, a big hand reached out of midair and grabbed Jarrah. A hand, an arm, and no body. And it was big enough to close its grip right around Jarrah.

Once again the stands fell silent. Because now they were finally seeing something even more important than the match.

The arm and hand began to withdraw into . . . into nothing, really. The hand had reached out of thin air. And it was drawing Jarrah away into thin air.

Dietmar was quickest and closest. He grabbed on to Jarrah's hand and held on tight. But the hand was still pulling, so Mack grabbed Dietmar, and Xiao grabbed Mack, and Stefan—who was an adorable eighteen inches tall—grabbed Xiao's ankle, and they all pulled back.

It was tug-of-war with an unseen god, which sounds like it might be the metaphorical title of a sermon, but in this case was a literal description of reality.

Jarrah slipped out of sight, drawn into nothing. But then she reappeared, pulled back.

Suddenly, the soccer players started getting into the act. They didn't like kids wandering around midfield, but they were even more opposed to giant hands. So they began to pummel the mighty god fingers and pull on Jarrah, and they kept it up until a gigantic wolf's head poked into view and roared so loudly, with such angry ferocity, that some pretty tough-looking guys lost their grip and ran screaming like little girls.

Only one player managed to hold on as Jarrah, Dietmar, Mack, Xiao, and tiny Stefan were yanked powerfully through the portal, to land in a disorganized heap on the floor of the observatory.

The hand did not belong to Thor as they had expected. It was mighty Odin's mighty hand. And Odin the mighty was mightily angry.

"I had a three-hundred-mark bet on that match!" Odin raged.

"You mean three thousand euros," Dietmar corrected him.

Odin blinked. He blinked again. Mack waited for the deathblow. As big and scary as Thor was, there was something about the very angry Odin that spelled out "No one messes with me!" in big, flashing neon letters. Odin looked old and worn down, but he looked like an old and worn-down version of a very scary guy you would not have wanted to meet when he was young and unworn.

In fact, Thor and Fenrir were hanging back and looking a bit nervous. After all, Odin might decide to blame them for this interruption in the match and the loss of his bet. Fenrir was chewing his paw, trying to look nonchalant, and Thor was paying a lot of attention to Mjolnir, which was now a guitar once more and apparently in need of polishing with Thor's sleeve.

Mack closed his eyes, prepared for death, and thought, Well, it was a good life. Short but good.

But when Mack looked again, he saw Odin's face transforming slowly from enraged mythological divinity to sheepish, starstruck fan.

Odin actually wiped a nervous hand on his tunic. He extended it to the soccer player, who stood gaping like your goldfish after you accidentally drop it on the carpet.

"You are . . . You are . . . Oh, by All-Father Me, you are Franz Müller! In the flesh! It is a great honor to meet you," Odin said. "I'm a huge fan."

The player extended a shaky hand and grasped two of Odin's salami-sized fingers.

"I saw you play for the national team against Spain when you scored three goals!" Odin enthused. "The greatest match I've seen in . . . well, I don't want to tell you how long; you'll think I'm—"

"A doddering old fool?"

For split second Mack was sure it was Dietmar. He didn't know Dietmar that well yet, but the kid had a distinct tendency to blurt out things that would be better kept to himself.

But it wasn't Dietmar.

Thor and Fenrir edged apart, and there she was in the space between them, striding forward with smirking confidence.

"Hel!" said Odin.

"Risky!" said Mack.

"You!" said Nott.

The daughter of the Pale Queen took a moment to pat Fenrir on his ruff.

Odin, who had seemed impossibly intimidating just seconds earlier, seemed to shrink and age as he gazed solemnly at the thin wisp of a girl.

There was no question who was more scared of who. Or whom. Whichever.

Or maybe there is a question, so let's clear up the hierarchy of fear: Odin was scared of Risky. Odin in turn scared Thor and Fenrir. Thor and Fenrir scared Nott.

And all of the above scared Mack. And none of the above scared Stefan, despite the fact that he was the size of a kitten. Jarrah lifted him up and cradled him in her arms protectively.

"So, Mack," Risky said, revealing her perfect teeth in a smile that was at least as warm as a penguin's feet and almost as inviting as a graveyard at midnight, "did you have a nice flight from China?"

"Wait," Thor said. But he said it politely. "We have a deal. I have your Magnifica. But before you take them, you have to pay me what you promised."

Even when he was shaking with fear, Mack noticed things. And he noticed just the slightest flicker in Risky's amazing green eyes.

"Yes, of course; we'll talk about it later."

Nott must have noticed something, too, because she said, "Don't trust her, you big oaf. She's lying."

Again a slight flicker, quickly hidden by a narrowing of the princess's eyes and a baring of her teeth, which grew sharp and long and positively vampirish. "I keep my bargains."

She snapped her fingers. The nearest of the pool-portals switched from the movie-theater view to a view of the park at the base of the Externsteine. More than a dozen blue-and-white police cars, and two orange-and-white ambulances, and a lot of cops and tourists—all agitated, many snapping pictures of the transformed monument, and some eating sandwiches—appeared and floated hologram-style.

There, in one corner, sucking on his oxygen while his flamboyantly dressed apprentice chatted with two girls, was Paddy "Nine Iron" Trout.

Risky's left arm began to grow. It stretched and turned serpentine. Or more accurately, octopoid (which is a real word). There were suckers lining the bottom of this fantastic appendage.

Risky extended her octo-arm into the hologram, wrapped it around Nine Iron, and pulled. He disappeared from the hologram and appeared, dazed and breathless, before them.

Risky didn't waste time on pleasantries or explanations. "Paddy, the money."

Nine Iron's eyes—yellowish and evil—flitted left and right. He gulped. He fumbled for his oxygen. And for just a moment Mack had the impression that Nine Iron was blushing. Like a little girl. A little girl with very bad skin.

"The money, Paddy," Risky said in a low voice.

"The money, is it?" Nine Iron stalled.

"Yes. The money."

"Ah, well, as to the money . . . My apprentice put it all on one of these newfangled cards."

"Your apprentice," Risky said.

"The lad with the pantaloons."

Using her octo-arm, Risky yanked Valin into the room.

"Gee-ah-ah-aaah!" Valin said upon seeing Odin, Thor, Nott, the Magnificent Four, the Asgard TV room, and Risky.

Risky held out her hand. Her actual hand. "The money."

Mack was pleased to see that Valin fumbled repeatedly in his effort to extract what turned out to be a debit card.

"What is this?" Odin demanded.

"It's the way they do things now," Risky said. She was clearly impatient. "Can I take my prisoners now?"

Odin looked unhappily at the card, turned it over, flicked it with his fingernail, and said, "Strange money."

"Yes, time marches on," Risky said. It was clearly a struggle for her to remain polite. But just as clearly, she didn't want to be distracted by a fight with Odin and the others. "It's the money, Odin. I don't lie."

"I doubt that," Dietmar said. "You are evil, and evil creatures would not hesitate to lie."

This time Mack kind of appreciated Dietmar's bluntness. Because Odin was obviously unconvinced, and Thor kept looking around anxiously, like he was waiting for someone or something.

Finally Thor asked, "Where are they?"

An impatient growl escaped from Risky's perfect white throat. "They are waiting for you," Risky said smoothly—too smoothly. "In fact, they are very excited to meet you, Thor."

"Are they?" The god of thunder looked pleased.

Mack smelled a rat. "Who?"

Thor grinned. "Led Zeppelin. I'm playing a real gig with Led Zeppelin."

Risky decided to bluff it through. "Yes, that's right, and the whole band is waiting for you to join them just as soon as I take care of this little bit of business."

"I don't think so," Mack said. "They've been broken up for years. And I think the drummer is dead!"

Risky struck, quick as a cobra. She leaped at Mack, teeth bared. Before he could so much as flinch, she had him in her powerful hands. "That's the last nerve I'm going to let you grind!"

"Throw me!" a squeaky voice cried.

A small yet shirtless muscular person flew through the air. Stefan landed on Risky's face, grabbed a perfectly sculpted eyebrow in each tiny hand, and kicked Risky in the teeth with his cute little feet.

"Get off me!" Risky screeched.

"You lied to me!" Thor raged.

"RUN!" Stefan bellowed. But it came out more like "Ruuuun!"

Mack ran. The others followed. Around the circular room they raced.

Risky grabbed Stefan and flung him like a rag doll. He twirled through the air as Jarrah cried, "Stefan!"

Stefan landed with a plop in the farthest of the pools and disappeared from view.

No choice now, Mack had to follow. He ran, shoved a paralyzed-with-horror Jarrah forward, cried, "Jump!" and plunged after Stefan.

He swooped through the bubble-membrane—

which if you were to make a compound word out of it would be a bubblebrane—and landed in a circle of tall stones.

Mack knew immediately where he was. He had seen pictures of it before.

Thirty-two

No one knows for sure what Stonehenge is for. But it was surely not built for what was now happening.

A brief pause while we consider Stonehenge. Stonehenge is a bunch of stones that form a henge. Of course that's not very helpful because no one knows what a henge is. So let's start over.

About, oh, five thousand years ago a bunch of primitive Britons decided they would like to make a big circle of stones. Why? No one knows. Maybe they were trying to build a sort of calendar. Today we create calendars out of paper and photos of Justin Bieber. But in those long-ago days they had no Justin Bieber because anyone who looked as cute and doe-like and vulnerable as Justin Bieber would have been barbecued.

Which, when you think about it . . . No, let's not go there.

Anyway, they dug a big circular ditch of stones. And then they probably danced and sacrificed some biebers to their pagan gods.

Flash forward a couple of thousand years, and now it's about three thousand years ago when a nameless, visionary pagan decided, "That old earthen circle is lame. We could totally build a much better one with stones. And then girls would like us."

"Brilliant!" the other pagans cried.

They set about building. They used really big stones, like fourteen feet tall. Or as they said back then, "about two shaquilles."

They built a nice circle of giant stones and topped them with giant horizontal stones, forming lintels.

And when you stood back and looked at it, you'd think, "You know, if we put a domed roof on this, it would look kind of like the Jefferson Memorial in Washington. Or like—"

And then the pagans might well sacrifice you for not knowing the difference between Neolithic and neoclassical architecture.

The pagans had no patience with architectural ignorance.

Once Stonehenge was built, they undoubtedly held a pagan dance, but a reserved, unathletic, somewhat awkward and rhythm-impaired dance because they were, after all, English.

The pagans enjoyed their big stone circle and brought their dates to see it. Until civilization came to Britain and all the pagans had to be killed off. Civilization didn't approve of pointless stone circles. Civilization didn't realize it could be a really great tourist attraction that would bring millions of visitors, each of whom would look around and ask, "What is it?"

In the intervening years, many of the giant stones were hauled off to make forts, castles, redoubts, and the other killing-related structures that civilization loves.

So now what the Magnificent Four had landed in the middle of was a puzzling, half-torn-down series of stone pi symbols.

And they were not alone. Ereskigal appeared just seconds behind them. And then Thor, and he was beyond berserk, because he was embarrassed and humiliated at having been played for a fool by Risky.

Stefan was in Jarrah's jeans pocket. His tiny head was barely able to peek out.

"Hey, I'm still shrinking!" a tiny voice cried.

Nine Iron and Valin dropped in next. Nine Iron drew the blade from his cane with the lightning quickness of a drunk turtle. But Valin was quicker. He had his knives out and was busy flashing them dramatically, slicing the air.

"You tricked me!" Thor thundered at Risky.

"You're really pathetic," Risky said, sneering openly at the thunder god.

Thor had Mjolnir in one hand, his sword in the other. "They are mine until you pay me what you promised."

"You want a piece of me?" Risky challenged.

"I got a hammer, and you look a lot like a nail," Thor shot back.

"Bring it, blondie," Risky snarled.

Jarrah pulled out her phone and began frantically dialing.

Xiao switched to dragon.

Dietmar yelled that everyone should be careful, Stonehenge was a priceless cultural treasure.

Mack measured the distance from where he stood to safety. But since Stonehenge is in the middle of nothing but farmland, he couldn't even guess which way to run.

"Mom?" Jarrah said into the phone, covering her ear with her hand to block the noise of Thor bellowing and Risky snarling and Mack whimpering and Nine Iron gasping for breath and Valin cheering himself on with admiring "Hah! Hee-yah!" sounds.

Thor hurled Mjolnir. It caught Risky in the stomach. She flew backward and smacked one of the rocks so hard the lintel was knocked loose.

It fell—tons of stone—on Risky's head.

But by the time it smashed down on her, she was

no longer her usual lusciously evil self. Instead she had become a giant, stocky woman with a long blond braid on one side of her head and a kind of twig ponytail on the other.

In fact, she looked half bad and half good. On the right side she was a blond Viking amazon—powerful, shiny, as healthy looking as a model in a yogurt commercial.

The left side of her looked like what the right side would look like if you killed it, buried it for a thousand years, and then dug it up. She was half alive and very Xena Warrior Princessish, and half animated corpse, complete with bits of exposed bone, hanging flesh tatters, and cavorting worms.

It was the corpse hand that stopped the lintel stone and tossed it aside as if it were no heavier than a Wheat Thin.

"Ah, now there's the Hel I know," Thor said. Mjolnir had returned to him.

"Yes, Mum, I know it's the middle of the night there," Jarrah shouted into her phone. "But I'm having a bit of a situation here and I need some Vargran words."

Valin advanced on Mack, still slashing away like he was cool. Mack was helpless. But Valin hesitated.

"Just surrender to Nine Iron, and I won't have to slice you up," Valin said.

"Maybe you're not a total cold-blooded killer," Mack said, hoping he was right.

"It's Stefan, Mum," Jarrah said. "I've shrunk him and he won't stop."

"Nice try," Valin said, and rushed at Mack.

Mack bolted.

Valin chased and Mack ran, weaving in and around the stones, dodging crazily. Mack was quick and had long experience fleeing. And Valin was slowed somewhat by his insistence on slashing away all ninjalike.

Risky held up her dead hand and grinned a grin that was half Crest whitening toothpaste and half the picture your dentist uses to scare you into flossing.

From her upraised clawlike hand shot not a beam but a sort of swirling mist of blue-black light. This struck Thor on his recently stabbed and hastily bandaged leg.

Thor cried out in pain. The deerskin leggings curled and crisped like plastic wrap in a fire. The skin beneath peeked through and then it, too, began to shrivel and boil with pustules that popped and oozed black goo.

But Thor wasn't done. He feinted, pretending to throw his hammer, but at the last minute he leaped high and stabbed downward with his sword.

Risky dodged, but too slowly, and the sword went through her stomach.

Shfoomp!

Unfortunately it cut the left side—the dead side, in case you've lost track—and rather than killing the evil princess, it released a swarm of spiders.

The spiders poured in a black and gray mass from the wound. Like some kind of hideous death vomit. Like the worst flavor of yogurt ever squishing out of a Go-Gurt tube. Like if you did time-lapse photographs of your nostrils over the entire course of a two-week cold. Except instead of mucus it was spiders.

The point is: spiders.

You may recall that Mack did not like spiders. He didn't like them the way dry straw doesn't like fire.

"Aaaah-ah-yaaaah!" Mack said.

He couldn't stop quickly enough and went

crunching crunching crunching across the spider stream.

Then Valin yelled, "Aaaah-ah-yaaaah!"

"Spiders!" Mack cried.

"Spiders!" Valin agreed.

And yet Valin would not stop chasing him and so Mack couldn't stop running and both of them were running and shrieking and alive with terror.

"You're breaking up," Jarrah said into her phone. "I can't use 'grow,' I already used it. I need, like, 'restore.' Please, Mum, hurry, I have to go! You're breaking up! Text me!"

Dietmar was unperturbed by the spiders. He waited patiently for Mack and Valin to do a complete panicky squealing circuit around the henge. Then, as they passed close by, he scooped up a handful of spiders and flung them at Valin.

That was it for Valin. He'd had enough. A person with arachnophobia may be able to stand stomping on them, but they sure can't stand having spiders in their embroidered jacket or their pantaloons.

Valin lost it and ran madly away, beating at his clothing like a crazy person.

Meanwhile, Nine Iron just about had his blade out.

"Thanks," Mack gasped to Dietmar.

Thor stumbled past as his pustulated leg folded beneath him. Risky was on him in a heartbeat. She yanked Thor's sword from her side and pressed the point against Thor's muscular throat.

"Oh, I'm just going to enjoy this," Risky said. She said it in a German/Scandinavian sort of accent so that *just* came out as *yoost* and *enjoy* sounded like *enyooooy*.

Because, see, she was in her Nordic goddess of the underworld mode.

Xiao flew up and up then dived and swooped between two of the stones, scraped beneath the lintel, and hit Risky in the back.

Risky toppled on top of Thor. She lost her grip on the sword.

"Hang on, Stefan!" Jarrah cried. "Hang on!"

" . . . . !" He said in a voice so tiny it can't be shown using visible letters.

Jarrah's phone made a fruity little chime indicating a text message.

Jarrah stared at her phone. And said, "Can that be right?"

Risky jumped up and slapped Xiao away with her dead hand. With a weary groan, she fumbled for and found Thor's sword. The thunder god looked too tired and stunned to do much about it.

Risky/Hel raised high the sword of Thor. And she smote him the deathblow!

Or would have. Except that at that moment Mack realized if Thor lost and Risky won, he, personally (and the whole world) was toast.

So in a moment of total crazy that was his own personal version of berserk, he grabbed Risky's braid (the blond one) and yanked her head back hard.

She spun around. Her face, half living beauty and half dead encrusted zombie, froze him to the marrow.

"I . . . ," he managed to sob. "I really should have taken some time to learn more Vargran."

That non sequitur gave Risky just a second's pause, during which Thor leaped, passed one arm around her neck and the other behind, and trapped her in the kind of headlock Stefan had often used on Mack.

Mack breathed a sigh of relief, retreated hastily away, tripped, fell hard on his back, and looked up dazed, only to find that Nine Iron had his blade out and pressed against Mack's very heart.

The problem was that although Nine Iron was slow, there wasn't really any way for Mack to move that didn't involve impaling himself.

"For the Pale Queen," Nine Iron croaked, and leaned forward. "And for my one true love!"

"Well, let's give it a birl," Jarrah said.

Thirty-three

Jarrah gave it a birl, which is Australian for "gave it a try."

"Arb harid fie-ma!" Jarrah shouted.

And instantly nothing happened.

"Arb harid fie-ma!" Jarrah cried again.

And still nothing.

"My *enlightened puissance* is run down!" Jarrah cried. Which was a sentence she had never imagined she'd say. "Mack! You try it!" Jarrah shouted.

Nine Iron said, "Now ends the . . ." He paused, fumbled with his free hand for his oxygen line.

"What is it again?" Mack cried.

"Arb harid fie-ma!"

". . . last hope of . . ." Nine Iron wheezed.

"Arg?"

"Arb!"

". . . humanity!"

"Arb harid fie-ma!" Mack cried.

And Nine Iron shoved the blade into . . . Well, we'll have to assume he shoved it into the ground. Because Mack was no longer staring up at a triumphant Nine Iron.

He was staring up at a tall, ghostly white woman with no eyes, mouth, nose, or hair. She had hands like flippers.

Mack blinked.

It was a mannequin.

A mannequin wearing a green dress and standing beside another mannequin wearing a purple dress.

Xiao was sprawled across a table piled with sweaters.

Dietmar stood nearby, blinking at the same mannequin as Mack.

Jarrah was still staring at her phone.

The four of them were in a department store. The women's department.

Xiao quickly resumed her human form.

The store did not seem to be open. There were no customers. No clerks. And the lights were low.

It would take some time for them to figure out what had happened. The short version is: it's best not to use magic words you don't know very well.

Because what Jarrah had asked her mother for were the words to say "Restore my friend," meaning "Return Stefan to his normal size." That would have been *Arb harut-ma*.

Whereas *harid* is the Vargran word for *store*. Not *re-store*. Just *store*.

And of course, since she'd yelled at her mother that she had to go, her mother had texted back the word *fie-ma*, which as we all know is the Vargran form of the verb "to go."

So what she had said in effect was "Friend store go!"

Her friend was now, in fact, in a store. All her friends were. They were all in a large London department store called Harrods. Which, to be fair, did sound a lot like *harid*.

We can't really blame Vargran for any of this. And on the plus side, the proper Vargran words, properly pronounced, did restore Stefan to normal size.

With two careful, delicate fingers, Jarrah drew a butterfly-sized Stefan from her pocket and set him atop a soft silk scarf.

She dialed her mother back and said, "One more time, eh?"

Once the store opened, they were able to buy a shirt for the newly normal-sized Stefan.

Mack's phone chirped for a text. He read,

> Mack, what should I wear?

Mack frowned and said, "What?" Then he texted,

> What?

And then the golem texted back the words that would strike terror into Mack's heart even from a distance of five thousand miles, and even after all he had endured.

CAMARO ASKED ME IF I KNOW HOW TO DANCE. I DO KNOW HOW TO DANCE. ALL GOLEMS CAN DANCE. ON THE FLOOR. ON THE WALLS. ON THE CEILING. IN FACT, WE CAN DETACH OUR LEGS AND LET THEM DANCE ALL BY THEMSELVES. I SAID, "YES." SO SHE SAID, "THEN YOU'RE GOING TO DANCE YOUR FEET OFF. SATURDAY NIGHT." THIS WORRIED ME BECAUSE AS I MENTIONED EARLIER, I GOT INTO TROUBLE WHEN I CAME TO SCHOOL WITHOUT FEET. I DECIDED TO CALL MACK, BUT HE DIDN'T ANSWER. SO I SENT HIM A TEXT.

2 the dance w/ Camaro. It's Friday night and I don't know what 2 wear.

Camaro wasn't making the golem dance. She had asked him to a dance. Camaro had always thought Mack was cute, and now . . .

"Mack, you look pale," Jarrah said.

"I'm dating Camaro," Mack said with a whimper. "She . . . she's built like Thor."

What good would it be saving the world if he got home someday only to find himself in a relationship with Camaro Angianelli?

They all stepped out of Harrods onto the street.

They headed down Victoria Street, walking off the terror, walking off the ickiness, trying to get their wits together. Every now and then Mack would mutter "Camaro" in a despairing tone.

But that was a problem for another day. Maybe, Mack reflected, the Magnificent Twelve would fail, the world would be conquered, and he would never have to find a way to break up with Camaro.

For now, it seemed he would have to get to the tomb of William Blisterthöng MacGuffin. And then dig him up. Which oddly enough did not sound as frightening as dating Camaro.

As they walked, they exchanged solemn vows that they would never let themselves be caught unprepared in such a deadly mess again.

They agreed that they should instantly move on to locating MacGuffin. They agreed that once they did that, it would be time to really buckle down and learn all the Vargran they could. And really understand the *enlightened puissance*.

"Okay, so we're agreed," Mack said.

"Absolutely," Jarrah said.

"We must find this second disk and study very hard," Dietmar said. "We don't know enough words."

"And we don't know all the rules," Xiao said. "Why was Jarrah unable to use the spell, but it worked when Mack said it? Only by learning can we hope to survive."

"And we have only thirty-three days left," Mack said grimly.

But then they reached the river Thames and saw the massive Ferris wheel called the London Eye.

"Huh," Stefan said.

"Cool, huh?" Mack said.

Dietmar said that they should very definitely

buckle down and study, not go off to ride some silly Ferris wheel.

It would be very stupid to go and play when they should be learning, Xiao said.

So they blew off studying and crossed the bridge to the Ferris wheel.

Which did end up being a very, very stupid choice. But that's another story.

THE DANCE WAS NOT AS MUCH FUN AS I HAD HOPED. CAMARO HAD TOLD ME TO WEAR SOMETHING LEATHER. SO I WORE TWO OF THE CUSHIONS FROM THE SOFA. NOW I HAVE TRIPLE DETENTION. ALSO I HAVE COUNSELING SESSIONS. MACK'S FATHER TOLD ME I NEED TO STRAIGHTEN UP AND FLY RIGHT. SO NOW I'M TRYING TO FIND ENOUGH MUD TO MAKE WINGS. I DON'T WANT MACK TO BE IN TROUBLE WHEN HE GETS HOME.

Opa-ma eb twif!

Turn the page for a sneak peek
at Mack's continuing adventures in
The Magnificent 12: The Key.

BOOK THREE
THE KEY

"Let me out of here, you crazy old man!" Mack cried.

"Ye'll ne'er lea' 'ere alive. Or at least ye wilnae be alive fur lang. Ha-ha-ha!" Which was Scottish, more or less, for, "You'll never leave here alive. Or at least you won't be alive for long. Ha-ha-ha!"

The Scots are known for butchering the English language and for their ingenuity with building things. The first steam engine? Scottish guy invented it. The first raincoat? A Scot invented that, too. The first television, telephone, bicycle—all invented by Scots.

They're a very handy race.

And the first catapult designed to hurl a twelve-year-old boy from the top of the tallest tower in a castle notable for its tall towers? It turns out that, too, was invented by a Scot, and his name was William Blisterthöng MacGuffin.

The twelve-year-old boy in question was David MacAvoy. All his friends called him Mack, and so did William Blisterthöng MacGuffin, although they were definitely not friends.

"Ye see, Mack, mah wee jimmy, whin ah cut th' rope, they stones, thare, whit we ca' th' counterweight, drop 'n' yank this end doon while at th' same time ye gang flying thro' th' air."

Mack did see this.

Actually the catapult was surprisingly easy to understand, although Mack had never been good at science. The catapult was shaped a little like a long-handled spoon that balanced on a backyard swing set. A rough-timbered basket full of massive granite rocks was attached to the short handle end of the spoon. The business end of the spoon, where it might have contained chicken noodle or minestrone, was filled with Mack.

Mack was tied up. He was a hog-tied little bundle of fear.

The spoon, er, catapult, had been cranked so that the rock end was in the air and the Mack end was down low. A rope held the Mack end down—a rope that twanged with the effort of holding all that weight in check. A rope whose short fibers were already popping out. A rope that looked rather old and frayed to begin with.

William Blisterthöng MacGuffin, a huge, burly, red-haired, red-bearded, red-eyebrowed, red-chest-haired, red-wrist-haired man in a plaid skirt[1] held a broadsword that could, with a single sweeping motion, cut the rope. Which would allow the rocks to swiftly drag down the short end of the spoon while hurling Mack through the air.

"Ye invaded mah privacy, uninvited, ye annoying besom. And now ye've drawn the yak o' th' Pale Queen, ye gowk!"

Or in decent, proper English, "You invaded my privacy uninvited, you annoying brat. And now you've drawn the eye of the Pale Queen, you ninny."

How far could the catapult throw Mack? Well, a well-made catapult . . . actually, you know what? This

---

[1] Okay, call it a kilt if you want; it still looks like a skirt.

particular kind of catapult is called a trebuchet. *Treh-boo-shay.* Let's use the proper vocabulary out of respect for Mack's imminent death.

A well-made trebuchet (this one looked pretty well made) can easily hurl 100 kilos (or approximately two Macks) a distance of 1,000 feet.

Let's picture 1,000 feet, shall we? It's three football fields. It's just a little less than if you laid the Empire State Building down flat. It's long enough that if you started screaming at the moment of launch, you'd have time to scream yourself out, take a deep breath, check your messages, and scream yourself out again.

That would be pretty bad.

Unfortunately it got worse. The castle tower was about three hundred feet tall. The castle itself sat perched precariously atop a spur of lichen-crusted rock that shot four hundred feet above the surrounding land.

So let's do the math. Three hundred feet plus 400 feet makes a 700-foot vertical drop. And the horizontal distance was about 1,000 feet.

At the end of all that math was a second ruined castle, which sat beside Loch Ness.

In Loch Ness was the Loch Ness monster. But

Mack wouldn't be hitting the lake, he'd be hitting the stone walls of that second castle, Urquhart Castle. He would hit it so hard his body would become part of the mortar between the stones of that castle.

"Dae ye huv ony lest words tae say afore ah murdurr ye?"

"Yes! I have last words to say before you murder me! Yes! My last words are: don't murder me!"

Mack could have used some magical words of Vargran. He was totally capable of doing it. Totally.

If.

If Mack had taken some time to study what words of Vargran had been given to him and his friends. Sadly, when Mack might have been studying he rode the London Eye Ferris wheel instead. And the next time he could have been studying he downloaded a game on his phone instead and played *Mage Gauntlet* for six hours. And the next time . . . Well, you get the idea.[2]

So instead of whipping out some well-chosen magical words, Mack could only say, "Seriously: please don't murder me."

Which is just pathetic.

Look, we all know Mack is the hero of the story. And

---

2 The moral of that story is: it's fun to play games on your phone! Wait, that can't be right.

we all know the hero can't be killed. So there's no way he's just going to be slammed into a ruined castle and—

"Cheerio the nou, ye scunner," MacGuffin said, and he swung the sword.

The blade parted the frayed rope.

But wait, seriously? Mack's going to die?

Gravity worked the way it usually does, and the big basket of rocks dropped like a big basket of rocks.

Hey! If Mack dies, the world is doomed and the Pale Queen wins!

"Aaaahhh!" Mack screamed.

He flew like a cannonball toward certain death.

Let's avert our gazes from the place and moment of impact.

No one wants to see what happens to a kid when he hits a stone wall—it's just too gruesome and disturbing. So let's back the story up a little and see how Mack got himself into this mess to begin with.

In fact, let's do some ellipses to signal that we are going back in time . . . to the day before . . .

Before . . .

"Ahhhhh!" Mack cried, gripping the dashboard. He was seated next to Stefan, who was driving.

"Aieeee!" Xiao cried, gripping the back of Mack's seat.

"Acchhh!" Dietmar cried, hugging himself and rocking back and forth.

"Yeee hah!" Jarrah shouted, flashing a huge grin as she pumped her fist in the seat behind Stefan.

A car—it happened to be yellow—roared straight for them, horn blaring, headlights flashing, driver forming his mouth into a terrified O shape.

Stefan jerked the wheel left and stomped on the gas. This was accidental. He had meant to stomp on the brakes but he was confused. He didn't really know how to drive.

"Other way, other way, otherwayotherwayother way—aaaaaaaahhhh!" Mack yelled as Stefan drove the rented car into a traffic circle.

Now, in most of the world the cars in a traffic circle go counterclockwise. The exceptions are England, Wales, Australia, New Zealand, Japan, a few other countries, and Scotland.

This happened to be a Scottish traffic circle.

Those of you who've read the first two books about the Magnificent Twelve may recall that our hero, Mack MacAvoy, was twelve years old. In fact, being twelve was an important part of being a member of the Magnificent Twelve. Because it wasn't just any random twelve people. It was twelve twelve-year-olds, each of whom possessed the *enlightened puissance*.

And remembering that, you might also be thinking, Who rents a car to a twelve-year-old?

Well, perhaps you're forgetting that Stefan was fifteen—although he was in the same grade as Mack. Stefan, not being one of the Magnificent Twelve, but more of a bodyguard, could have been any age. He happened to be fifteen, and he looked eighteen. Which is still not old enough to be renting a car. Especially when you don't have a driver's license.

But you may also remember the part about Mack being given a million-dollar credit card.

Cost of car rental: 229.64 GBP.[3]

Cost of the gift certificate to Jenners department store in Edinburgh in the name of the car-rental clerk: 3,000.00 GBP.

Yeah: it's amazing what you can do with a million dollars. Renting a car is the least of it.

"There's a truck!" Mack shouted.

"It's called a lorry here!" Dietmar yelled in his know-it-all way.

"I don't care if it's called a—"

"Jog a little to the right there," Jarrah suggested

---

3 GBP means Great British Pounds. It's like money, but with pictures of the queen.

quite calmly, and put her hand on Stefan's powerful shoulder. Stefan did as he was told.

The truck or lorry or whatever it was called let go a horn blast that could have shattered a plate glass window and went shooting past so close that, *bang*, it knocked the left side mirror off the little red car.

"The mirror!" Xiao cried.

"Enh," Stefan said, and shrugged. "I wasn't using it anyway."

He wasn't. As far as Mack could tell, Stefan wasn't even using the windows, let alone the mirrors, and was more or less driving according to some suicidal instinct.

The car had seemed like a bad idea from the start, but Mack didn't like to come across all bossy, or like he was a wimp or something. One of the problems with having twenty-one identified phobias—irrational fears—is that people tend to think you're a coward. Mack was not a coward: he just had phobias. Which meant there were twenty-one things he was cowardly about—tight spaces, sharks, needles, oceans, beards, and a few others—but he was brave enough about most things.

So when it had been pointed out to him that having made it by train from London to Edinburgh,

Scotland, the best way to get from there to Loch Ness was by car, he'd gone along. To demonstrate that he was not a huge wimp.

How was that going? Like this:

"Gaaa-aah-ahh!" Dietmar commented.

BAM!

Rattle rattle rattle rattle.

Thump!

The car hit the low curb guarding the center of the circle, bounced over the lumpy grass, swerved around some sort of monument, narrowly missed a pair of Mini Coopers—one red, one tan—and bounced out of the other side of the circle and onto the main road.

Mack, Xiao, and Dietmar all took the first breath they'd inhaled in several minutes.

Stefan said, "Is there a drive-through in this country? I'm starving."

And Jarrah said, "I'm so hungry I could eat a horse and chase the jockey."

Jarrah and Stefan: obviously they were not quite normal.

Having survived the traffic circle, the gang found a gas station that also had food. They bought prepackaged sandwiches and sodas. They topped the car off with gas. And that's when Mack noticed a van he had noticed earlier. There was nothing remarkable about the van—it was beige, which is the world's least noticeable color. But Mack was a kid who noticed things and he noticed that this van had a dent on one side. A small thing. But what were the odds that there were two tan vans with the same dent?

He had first noticed this van way back just outside Edinburgh, and now that Mack looked closer, it seemed the windshield was tinted. Which would be a perfectly normal thing where Mack was from—the Arizona desert, where the sun shone 360 out of 365 days—but was pretty strange here in Scotland, where the sun shone 5 days out of 365.

"That van has been following us," Mack said as the five of them leaned against their car eating.

No one questioned him. They'd all learned that when Mack noticed something, he noticed it right.

So they leaned there and watched the van. Which maybe was watching them back.